MW01132849

TANGLED UP IN LOVE

CHARLOTTE BYRD

Epic love requires an epic sacrifice...

A long time ago, I borrowed money from a very powerful family. I paid my debt, but they have come for more.

They want everything that I have built and they will hurt her if I refuse.

Harley doesn't understand why I have to break her heart. She hates me, but at least she's okay...for now.

But what happens when sending her away isn't enough?

What happens when I lose everything?

PRAISE FOR CHARLOTTE BYRD

"Decadent, delicious, & dangerously addictive!" - Amazon Review ★★★★★

"Titillation so masterfully woven, no reader can resist its pull. A MUST-BUY!" - Bobbi Koe, Amazon Review ★★★★★

"Captivating!" - Crystal Jones, Amazon Review ★★★★★

"Exciting, intense, sensual" - Rock, Amazon Reviewer ★★★★★

"Sexy, secretive, pulsating chemistry..." - Mrs. K, Amazon Reviewer ★★★★★

"Charlotte Byrd is a brilliant writer. I've read loads and I've laughed and cried. She writes a balanced book with brilliant characters. Well done!" - Amazon Review ★★★★★

"Fast-paced, dark, addictive, and compelling" - Amazon Reviewer ★★★★★

"Hot, steamy, and a great storyline." - Christine Reese ★★★★★

"My oh my....Charlotte has made me a fan for life." - JJ, Amazon Reviewer ★★★★★

"The tension and chemistry is at five alarm level." - Sharon, Amazon reviewer ★★★★★

"Hot, sexy, intriguing journey of Elli and Mr. Aiden Black. - Robin Langelier ★★★★★

"Wow. Just wow. Charlotte Byrd leaves me speechless and humble... It definitely kept me on the edge of my seat. Once you pick it up, you won't put it down." - Amazon Review ★★★★★

"Sexy, steamy and captivating!" - Charmaine, Amazon Reviewer ★★★★★

" Intrigue, lust, and great characters...what more could you ask for?!" - Dragonfly Lady ★★★★★

"An awesome book. Extremely entertaining, captivating and interesting sexy read. I could not put it down." - Kim F, Amazon Reviewer ★★★★★

"Just the absolute best story. Everything I like to read about and more. Such a great story I will read again and again. A keeper!!" - Wendy Ballard
★★★★★

"It had the perfect amount of twists and turns. I instantaneously bonded with the heroine and of course Mr. Black. YUM. It's sexy, it's sassy, it's steamy. It's everything." - Khardine Gray, Bestselling Romance Author ★★★★★

DON'T MISS OUT!

Want to be the first to know about my upcoming sales, new releases and exclusive giveaways?

Sign up for my Newsletter and join my Reader Club!

Bonus Points: Follow me on BookBub!

ALSO BY CHARLOTTE BYRD

All books are available at ALL major retailers! If you can't find it, please email me at charlotte@charlotte-byrd.com

Black Series
Black Edge
Black Rules
Black Bounds
Black Contract
Black Limit

Lavish Trilogy
Lavish Lies
Lavish Betrayal
Lavish Obsession

Tangled Series

Tangled up in Ice

Tangled up in Pain

Tangled up in Lace

Tangled up in Hate

Tangled up in Love

Standalone Novels

Debt

Offer

Unknown

Dressing Mr. Dalton

DEDICATION

This book is dedicated to all parents who have lost children before birth...You are not alone.

1
———————

JACKSON

Long before...

Y ou walk into the bathroom where the light
pours in through the skylight, creating a
glow around your head as if you are the angel that I
know you to be.

You run your fingertips over the vanity,
enjoying the smoothness of the marble.

Your nails are Color Therapy's *Ohm My
Magenta*, and it's your favorite polish.

You paint them yourself and you don't care that
it peels off within a few days.

In fact, you like it.

A big part of why you paint them yourself is

that you are a recovering nail-biter, so now you focus your energy on picking at your nails instead of biting them.

A few of them are long, past your fingertips, but the ring finger on your left hand is the most recent victim of late night biting.

Of course, I don't know any of these things when you walk up to me.

I don't know anything about you except for how you make me feel. My stomach is in knots.

My palms are sweaty.

My throat is tight.

You pick up the scissors and hold them steady in your hand.

They are professional hairdressing scissors, but you aren't afraid of them.

This isn't your first time holding a pair like that.

"Have you done this before?" I ask.

My voice cracks a little on the second word, but I clear it quickly and continue.

Our eyes meet.

Yours are hazel and wide.

There's a line of charcoal eyeliner just along the top lid. It goes a little past your eye, but not high enough to give you a cat eye.

Your lashes are painted in mascara, making them fuller and slightly longer than they would be naturally.

Your makeup is light, and accentuating.

At no point does it cover up who you are and that's what I like best about it.

"I've never cut a man's hair."

You answer my question without really answering it.

"Do you cut your own?"

You blush. You look away. I nod and sit back, giving you space.

"Yes." You finally admit.

I know that you are embarrassed by this, but I don't want to call you on it. We don't know each other well.

"It's just so...stupid," you say.

"What?"

"I shouldn't be telling you this...but, yes, I do cut my own hair."

"Why?" I ask, leaning back on the closed toilet lid that I'm perched on.

"Because it costs a fortune to go to a hair stylist in New York. And when I was a teenager, I didn't have any money, not that that's really different now. Anyway, I didn't want to spend the little money that I had on paying someone to trim my hair. So, I learned to do it myself."

You are talking so fast, I am surprised that you are not out of breath.

"I just wear it long, like this. Sometimes a bit

shorter. The only thing I really do is trim it a bit. It's not that complicated to do yourself." You continue to explain.

I smile at the corners of my mouth.

"What?" You ask.

"I didn't ask why you do it yourself. What I meant was why shouldn't you be telling me this?"

This takes you aback. You shrug your shoulders and look down at the floor. Instead of large slabs of contemporary tile like in the rest of the house, I wanted to keep this bathroom as authentic to the origins of the house as possible.

Tiny, small tiles line up in exquisite patterns with nearly invisible grout.

It's still there, of course, and I'm sure that it's a headache for the housekeepers to clean.

"I'm not sure," you say. "We don't really know each other that well, I guess."

"I'd like to get to know you more."

You blush again. I don't want to come on too strong, but I need you to know. I lean back again and give you space.

You take a step closer to me and place your hands on my head.

Shivers run down my spine.

I inhale slowly, so that you don't see how nervous I really am. It's important to stay cool at times like this.

You are timid and scared enough, and I don't want to frighten you. What I need you to know is that I'm scared, too.

One day, we'll tell each other about this moment and laugh.

But not today.

"So, how do you want it?" you ask.

I've cut it recently, but it wasn't short enough.

"I don't want it too short, of course, just sort of like the way it is, only a bit shorter."

You nod.

Your hands are in my hair, feeling the strands.

Every time you make a move, my whole body yearns for yours.

I want you to tug and pull hard, so that I can feel more.

But you are gentle and careful.

Your eyes focus entirely on the task at hand.

You pick up a strand of hair and snip off the end.

Even though you are afraid of making mistakes, who isn't, you begin. I appreciate that. I trust you.

Of course, it can end badly, but I don't care. It's just hair. If you cut it too short, I'll cut it shorter and fix what I can.

What I have now is enough. I want this moment to last as long as possible.

You examine my hair.

You feel its texture.

You hold the strand across your index and middle fingers.

You spread out the strand and cut vertically toward your fingers.

You are no expert, but you are no amateur either. You are wearing a thick gray sweater that opens down the middle, layered over a long-sleeve V-neck. You look cozy and warm, but I know that you're not.

Your fingers touching my scalp are as cold as ice.

"Is it too cold in here? I can turn the thermostat up."

"Yeah, I'd love that. I get cold easily."

"No problem."

I reach for my phone, press a few buttons, and hot air starts to pump into the room.

I hope it gets warm enough here for you to take off the top layer.

"Thank you." You whisper. Your eyes only briefly focus on mine and then quickly dart back to the job at hand.

As you make your way around my head, and position yourself right in front of my face, I let my eyes drift down from your eyes toward your breasts.

I don't know this yet, but you hate wearing bras.

You don't like the way they pinch your back. You don't like the padded ones because they push them too high, your words not mine, and you don't like the ones with the underwire because they dig into your sides.

Your breasts aren't very big, but their size is perfect to fit exactly into my palms.

The only ones you find moderately acceptable are the bralettes that are basically a cloth of lace that hold you up a bit.

Today, you are wearing a t-shirt bra, with no underwire, but with plenty of padding.

I'll later learn that this is the one you wear to important meetings and events, even though it's light blue and not at all fancy.

I'll also later learn that you take off your bra as soon as you get home and if you are going nowhere special like a grocery store or running another errand, you will not wear a bra at all.

"Okay, what about this?" You say, pulling away from me and pointing me to the mirror.

"It's...perfect," I say slowly, feeling the ends of my hair where your fingers have been.

"Really?" You don't believe it. "You don't want me to fix up some parts? Just let me know if you think some are too short or too long."

"No," I say, shaking my head. "I love it."

2

JACKSON

NOW...

I sit next to her in the dark hospital room.
I am sitting on the couch near the windowsill, looking out of the fifth floor window onto the street below.

The street is drenched in light and life, the opposite of this room. Harley faces away from me.

She is curled up in the fetal position, she runs her fingers over the space between the pillow and the sheet over and over again. She is here and she's not here. Awake and asleep.

I have tried talking to her before and I will try again.

But for now, I let her be. I don't know how long we have to be here, if at all. I want to ask, but I don't have the energy to do a single thing but to sit here and stare out at the world below.

An ambulance rushes down the street with the horn blasting.

It goes around the corner toward the emergency entrance out of sight.

Someone is hurt. Someone is dying. Someone is losing something.

I reach over to the glass.

I press my palm against it. It's warm outside, sticky and humid, but the glass still feels cold against my touch.

I hold my hand against it, enjoying the sensation of my fingers being spread open and the blood draining away from them.

How is it that we were so happy only a few hours ago?

Anger starts to rise up within me as my thoughts drift back to what happened right after we left the restaurant.

The thoughts come to me in pieces and then all at once. Julie was in the car, and I got behind the wheel.

Martin was waiting for Harley to get into the back when someone on a bicycle came up to him and shot him in the head.

He was a blur of darkness riding past us. I only heard the sound and then it was all over.

A bullet had launched itself in Martin's head. His life vanished in a moment.

But that wasn't all.

The man on the bicycle plowed into Harley. He threw her into the air and she fell on the pavement.

He was climbing back onto the bike when I got to her.

I had the choice to stay with her and with Martin or chase him down. And my split-second decision will now haunt me for the rest of my life.

Another ambulance screeches around the corner. I glance back at Harley. She doesn't make a move.

I watch her breathe.

One breath comes in, another goes out.

Not hurried.

Not out of control.

But not particularly calm either.

She is detached. Her body is here, but she is somewhere else altogether.

Instead of trying to chase down the man who shot Martin and threw her over his handlebars, I stayed with them.

I regret this, but then...what else could I do?

She landed on her stomach and her eyes rolled back into her head. She wasn't there and I couldn't just leave her.

Martin was dead and if I left her, she might die, too.

When the ambulance arrived, they placed her

into the back and refused to let me inside. I didn't even bother asking Julie if she wanted to come.

She draped herself over Martin, taking turns sobbing and screaming into his ear.

I drove the car straight here and left it in the front of the hospital with the doors open and the keys inside.

It's probably towed, as if I give a shit.

Instead of letting me right back to see Harley, they first forced me to fill out pages of paperwork.

They don't show this in the movies, but that's what I had to do rather than be with her.

"Just sit down and focus on this," the nurse said, handing me the clipboard.

"I'll pay whatever the bill is, I don't care about the insurance. Just let me in there to see her."

"I am sorry, sir, but everyone has to follow the protocol."

So, that's what I was doing. I was answering questions on a piece of paper while our baby was dying.

3

JACKSON

IN THE SILENCE...

You'd think that the hospital room would be quiet, but it's not.

One of the machines puts out a low buzzing sound and another one beeps sporadically.

The door is closed, but the voices from the outside come in loud and clear.

The nurses are laughing and gossiping about their boyfriends. I wish I could turn on the light to make this moment seem a bit more real, but Harley doesn't want it on. She just wants to lie in here in almost darkness.

I finally pull myself from the window and reach for the remote control. I need something to distract me.

My thoughts keep going back to that moment

when I learned my baby was gone, and if I don't do something soon, I know they will suffocate me.

"No, keep that off," Harley says when I flip on the television.

It's the first time that she has said anything to me this whole evening. It's the first thing that she has said to me since she got into the ambulance.

"I need something on to...not think about it anymore."

"You don't want to think about it anymore?" she asks without turning around.

She is being cruel.

I know this. She is focusing her anger at me because there's no one else here. But still it hurts.

I turn off the television and the room returns to darkness.

The voices outside the room pick up.

After a few minutes, my eyes adjust and I return my gaze to the street. I give in because I feel like I lost a lot more than she did. But I lost just as much. We both lost our child.

Time passes as if it's standing still. I stare at the dirty glass, full of my fingerprints. With every moment, I descend further into darkness. It's calling me. It's whispering my name. Just let go. Stop fighting. Come here. It's all going to be okay once you are here.

My phone vibrates.

It's a text message from Phillips. She's putting out another fire at Minetta.

My job seems like it's the last thing I should worry about right now but thinking about it somehow takes some of the pain away.

I text her back. The physical act of typing and thinking actually alleviates some of the pain. It's more than a distraction. It's a lifeline.

Once I send the text, I open my email. There are more problems to deal with. I let out a sigh of relief.

I can't make myself or Harley feel better, but I can do this.

This will make me forget. I know it will because that's exactly what I did when I lost Lila.

No matter what, I will not compare the pain of losing them. It's not fair to either. Lila was a child.

She had a personality I knew.

She had years of my life invested in her.

This baby was real but not, at the same time. I don't know who she or he would've been.

I don't know what they would've been like. All I know is that this baby was my second chance to love a little creature again. And now, that chance is gone.

After answering eight emails, I glance over the phone at Harley. At first, everything is pitch black.

With my screen so bright, I don't see a thing.

But as my eyes adjust, they meet hers. She has turned around and is now facing me.

Her body is still in the same fetal position with the blanket wrapped firmly around her shoulders.

She's looking at me without blinking.

"How are you?" I ask, immediately regretting the banality of this question. But what else is there to ask? Say?

She doesn't respond.

That's when it hits me. She's not looking at me, but past me. Her eyes look at something in the distance, which is far over my head.

"Harley," I say. Her name seems foreign in my mouth. It's as if I hadn't said it before.

"I am so sorry," I say. My words crack. Tears start to well up in my eyes. My throat closes up.

She takes the blanket and turns around under it. Her face doesn't change in expression a bit.

I am certain that she is now staring out in the distance on her other side just like she did here.

At a loss as to what to do next, I return to my phone.

After Lila died, I grew this company to what it is today without much help from anyone else. I spent all of my waking days working and it was only then that my wounds learned to heal.

Or maybe the work just distracted me from the pain?

Maybe I'm not over Lila's death at all.

Can a parent ever get over the loss of a child? Is it foolish to even contemplate such a thing?

Somewhere in the back of my inbox, I find an old email that I never opened. It's about all the money that I lost in the financial fraud scam.

Not long ago, I would've paused over it and hesitated opening it. But tonight, I couldn't care less. I click on it and read the contents.

It's from one of the prosecutors in charge of the case and it's not good news. Apparently, the family had spent most of the money that they stole and it's unlikely that anyone will get paid back anything.

I close it without another thought.

Who the hell cares about all of those millions of dollars?

I should, perhaps, but right now I can't summon the strength to give a shit even a little bit.

The news makes me chuckle.

"Are you laughing?" Harley asks, turning around surprised.

I shrug my shoulders and point to the phone. She knows about the money and she knows how much I wanted to get it back.

"That money I got swindled out of...it's pretty much all gone."

"It was gone."

"Yeah, but I always held on to a little hope that

I'd be able to get it back and use it to get a controlling interest in Minetta again."

They paid me more than Minetta is worth, of course, but maybe I could pay them even more to get my rightful percentage back.

"I guess that's out." I laugh again.

She shrugs.

"How can you think about work at a time like this?"

What else is there to think about, I ask her silently.

HARLEY

IN THE DARKNESS...

J ackson taps on the window. Jackson turns on the television. Jackson answers emails and texts on his phone.

Jackson annoys me.

Why can't he just be?

Why can't he just relax and calm down?

I want to throw the pillow at him, but that would require getting up and actually engaging my body.

The prospect of that is impossible.

I feel like there's a heavy object that's laying on top of me that I cannot move. Even to turn from one side of the bed to the other requires a Herculean effort.

I keep my eyes open because when I close

them, I see Martin's. Just a moment ago, they were so full of life.

I didn't know him well, but whenever we spent time together, he put me at ease. He was easy to talk to and he loved Julie.

And more than that even, he made her happy.

Blood is streaming down one side of his face, following the edge at first and then dripping straight down onto the ground.

His eyes are glassy, vanquished of all life. The hole in his forehead is dark and deep.

I reach for him, and he is only a bit out of my grasp.

Please come back, I say to myself. Please come back. You can't leave. You can't be...dead.

All of this happens in a second.

A mere glimpse. Just a moment.

That's when the pain sets in.

As I lay there, looking at the body of my friend who died trying to protect me, my arm starts to throb. A strong shooting pain runs up my body and centers in my shoulder, in the place where I landed.

I don't know exactly what happened yet, or how I ended up on the ground. When I search my mind for that no memories emerge.

All I remember is standing next to him and

hearing a loud popping sound that I thought belonged to a car backfiring.

What happened next, I don't exactly know.

Suddenly, I am lying on the ground gazing into Martin's eyes.

My shoulder starts to throb, but that pain is manageable. The one that follows it isn't. It's come from the center of my core.

I grab my stomach to try to help my baby, but the pain gets worse and worse. Warm liquid starts to pool in between my legs and tears of pain, regret, and anger roll down my cheeks.

"Stay, stay, stay," I whisper under my breath. "It's going to be okay."

Suddenly, Jackson is there. He's holding me, promising me impossible things. Sirens are blaring in the distance.

The ambulance is almost here.

I promise the same impossible things to the baby. I try to breathe through the pain, but it doesn't help. I pray for this to stop.

When they lift me up onto the stretcher, I look over at Martin.

Julie is on top of him, her sobs are echoing around the buildings. I've never seen her like this, but then again, I've never seen someone get shot before either.

Jackson fights to come inside the ambulance

with me but they won't let him. They physically push him out of the back, and a part of me is relieved. This is all my fault.

Our baby is dead because of me.

The police will need evidence to find out who did it, but I don't.

I know it's Parker. Or at the very least, it's someone he hired. If he can't have me, then he will kill me. Only problem is that I survived and my friend and my baby are dead.

My hopes that things did not turn out as the worst case scenario aren't dashed until we get to the hospital.

All throughout that ambulance ride, I still believe that it's going to be okay. I still have hope.

But then the pain gets worse and they take me into one of the rooms.

They try to make the bleeding stop but it's too late. The baby is too young. It's still a collection of cells. And my body is weak.

"Luckily, you will still be able to have children," a man in a white coat says.

Lucky is not what I would describe myself as, I think to myself. And that sentence should be *other* children. I'm not lucky enough to have this one.

A KNOCK on the door startles me, but I barely move. Jackson goes to see who it is. I hope it's not Julie. I can't bear to see her yet. I'm not sure if I ever will be ready even though I know that I will have to.

"Thanks for coming." I hear Jackson say.

With great difficulty, I move under the heavy weight that's smushing me into the bed to face the door.

The hallway is bright and full of stomping feet and loud voices, and I can't quite see who is at the door.

Jackson wraps his arms around the visitor and I want to throw up. I can't see her face, but I sense that it's Aurora.

Who else could it be? And now, look at her, hugging Jackson, trying to be there for him. I don't really have anything against her but I am not a big fan of how close they are and how he's always there for her.

I turn away from the door and pull my blanket above my head to try to drown their whispers out completely.

Why isn't the fucking television on when you need it to be?

"Harley! Honey!" A familiar voice rushes over to me.

She falls on top of me, shielding me from the

weight that's been keeping me in this bed by her body.

"What are you doing here?" I ask, my voice cracking.

"I'm here, honey. We both are."

Tears start to stream down my face. She pulls away briefly, giving my dad some space to get in on the hug.

"Mom...Dad..." My voice trails off and I am suddenly ten years old again, crying in my parents' arms, waiting for them to make everything fine again.

5

HARLEY

My parents hold me for a while and don't pull away until I do.

They are just there for me.

They don't bombard me with questions of how I am or what I'm feeling. They just wait. I appreciate it.

While they hold me, Jackson stands back and waits. I don't know exactly how much time passes, but after a while I start to feel hot and I push them away in order to get some fresh air.

Jackson pulls over two chairs from the other side of the room and sits back down on the couch which he has made into his sanctuary.

Out of the corner of my eye, I see him toying with the idea of wrapping his feet in a blanket just like he did before.

The room is not particularly warm but he pushes the blanket away, deciding against it.

Once my parents pull away from me and pull their seats to the edge of my bed, Jackson asks if he can put on the light.

"Yes, of course," Mom says immediately. But Jackson waits for me to respond.

"It's just that the light was bothering her before," he explains.

"Oh, sure, whatever you want, honey," Dad says.

"Is there any way to not have the big one on overhead?"

Jackson scours the room and then finds the switch to the smaller light above the bed, but it's somehow even more oppressive. Instead of a neutral color, this one drenches everyone in a horrible fluorescent green.

"Okay, just put the big one on, it's fine."

As much as I want to hide in blackness, I don't want to force everyone to sit in the dark.

"So, you called them, huh?" I ask Jackson. He shrugs and nods.

"And got us a plane to bring us here."

"Really?"

"I have to say, a private plane is the way to go," Dad says. He's not being obtuse or rude, he's just trying to lighten the mood. And I appreciate that.

With great difficulty and a foldable hospital bed, I manage to sit up.

"It is pretty nice," I agree. "Thank you," I say, turning to Jackson. Again, he just shrugs and looks down at the floor.

"So...how are you?" Mom asks. Now it's my turn to nod and hang my shoulders.

"I don't know," I mumble.

I glance past my parents to Jackson.

Suddenly, it occurs to me that I don't know if they *know*.

I mean, they know about Martin and how I almost got killed, but I don't know if Jackson told them about my pregnancy.

I certainly did not.

"So, how's everything going?" I ask, trying to change the topic. "You're newlyweds again, right?"

They exchange glances and can't help but smile at each other.

"We are just so happy you're okay," Mom says, taking my hand in hers. "We were so scared."

"I know."

They don't say anything for a few moments.

"Are you going to answer my question?"

"We're doing really well," Dad says. "We're really happy."

I smile at him. "That's good. I'm glad."

"And thank you and Jackson so much for the ranch, of course," Mom says.

I stare at her. What is she talking about?

I glance over at Jackson but he avoids eye contact with me.

"What do you mean?" I ask.

"For giving us the money to rebuild the ranch," Dad explains. "We really appreciate it. And we're going to pay you every cent of it back, Jackson. Please believe us."

"You really don't have to," he mumbles.

Thoughts rush through my mind so fast, I get dizzy. Why didn't he tell me about this? Why didn't they? Why did he give them the money?

"Why didn't you tell me?" I ask him. I probably should've waited until we were alone to ask him, but I'm tired of secrets. There has been more than enough of them among all of us. I don't want to keep another one.

"You didn't know?" my dad asks, surprised.

"No."

"It was always their dream so after the wedding, I just gave them a check to rebuild what they had lost. That's it."

"It was so...generous. We just can't thank you enough."

"Was this before or after you dumped me?" I

ask. I don't know why but for some reason I am fuming.

I'm angry at him for giving them the money. I'm angry at them for accepting it. But mostly, I am just angry. Under the fluorescent lights, my anger intensifies and I can't hide below the surface for much longer.

"You and Jackson broke up?" Dad asks.

"Are you back together?" Mom pipes in.

"No, we didn't break up. Jackson broke up with me."

"But now...everything is fine?" Mom asks again.

"No, Mom, everything is not fine."

I feel like I'm drowning. Seeing them here, talking about the ranch, thinking about my baby, it's just all too much. I can't handle it. Tears start to run down my face faster than I can wipe them off.

"Please...leave...I can't...do this anymore."

My parents try to comfort me again, but it just makes things worse. Eventually, Jackson manages to push them out of the door.

"If you ask if I'm okay, I'm going to scream," I warn him when he turns off the lights.

He nods and sits down in my mom's chair, taking my hand in his. I want to push him away, but I don't.

6
_____

JACKSON

WHEN WE GIVE HER SPACE...

I've always thought that the coffee in a hospital would come from a vending machine, along with stale M&M's that crack in two halves as soon as I bite down on them even a little bit.

But when I head downstairs to get Harley some tea, I am pleasantly surprised to find a beautiful Starbucks with a quirky green couch and plenty of millennials glued to their laptops at the bar.

It's almost as if this place is in West Village rather than a hospital.

I get behind two young doctors who look like they've worked a thirty-hour shift. When one of them grabs her latte, she laughs and says that she needs to have this put into an IV drip.

The other one asks for a green tea and mentions that too much caffeine makes her jittery.

I see Harley's parents sitting by the window at the far end of the coffee shop and they wave me over.

I gesture that I have to get my drink first and secretly hope that it takes as long as possible.

It's not that I don't want to see them or talk to them.

It's that I don't really know how much I should or shouldn't say about the true nature of Harley's condition.

I know that she did not tell them about the baby and I don't feel like it's my place to tell them.

Yet, I have grown close to them throughout everything that we have been through. And that makes me feel like by not telling them the truth that I am lying.

I order an espresso, two shots.

Since I'm going to drink it with them, I decide to order her tea when I'm about to head back up.

"Thanks for coming," I say, sitting down at the end of a square table. Harold and Leslie are sitting across from one another, nursing their drinks.

"Thank you for telling us. And for the flight, of course," Harold says.

A half-eaten croissant rests in the middle of the table. Leslie offers me some, but Harold asks if he can get me my own. I decline both offers.

"It's the least I could do."

"No, the least you could've done is not bother calling us at all, not booking us on a private plane leaving an hour after the call," Harold points out. It sounds like a joke, but I don't think it is.

"You are Harley's parents and I consider you...family."

The word takes me by as much of a surprise as it seems to take them.

Leslie wipes her eye with the back of her hand, placing her other on mine and giving it a small squeeze.

Unsure as to what we should talk about besides the reason why we are here, I ask them about work.

"Busy as always," Leslie says. "The police department doesn't exactly run itself."

"I'm glad you were able to get time off to come here."

"I wouldn't have it any other way."

"What about you, Harold?"

"The kids are keeping me busy."

"You're back to teaching?"

"Retirement isn't exactly my thing. There was an opening for a substitute. It was only supposed to last a week but the teacher is having some personal problems so I'll be filling in for her until next year."

"Are you happy to be busy?"

"Of course. Besides, it's not like I have much to come back to. My new wife here tends to work over eighty hours a week."

Leslie smiles at him and I can feel the love that emanates from both of them.

"So, what about the ranch? Any plans yet?"

"Oh my God, of course!" Leslie says excitedly. "We had plans drawn up and we're going to build it to look just like the old house. An exact replica."

"Wow, that's...brave."

Perhaps, there's a better word for it but one doesn't come to mind.

A long time ago, they lost everything they ever loved there.

It wasn't the physical house that they had lost.

No, that fire also took their youngest child, their marriage, and even a relationship with their older child.

Not everyone would pick at those wounds again in their position. But Leslie and Harold are stronger than they may even know.

They dared to take a chance on each other again and through this love they were able to reconnect with Harley.

And now, they are rebuilding their dream once again.

"Thank you for that, Jackson. Thank you very

much," Harold says. "It means a lot that you see what we are doing."

The conversation drifts to other topics including my work and the weather. It seems as though we will talk about just about anything, except Harley.

Finally, Harold broaches the subject and I repeat what I told them on speakerphone when I first called.

I go over the scene in as much detail as I can, mainly for Leslie's sake.

I know that she is looking at this as a law enforcement officer with many years of experience.

So, the more I tell her, the more useful she can be.

"Can you describe the man on the bike?" Leslie asks me. She had already asked this question in a few different ways before but I answer it again without a tinge of annoyance.

"Slender or thin. He was wearing all black clothing. His face was covered in a ski mask. Black also. I only saw him get on the bike so I didn't get a good look when he was right there."

"Do you think it was Parker?"

"He looks like the man who I saw, but I can't say for sure. What I do know for sure is that he was behind this."

"How do you know?" Leslie asks.

"He's the one who has been stalking her. Who else would it be?"

"But why did he kill Martin?" Harold asks.

7

JACKSON

WHEN I EXPLAIN...

I stare at him. I have no answer to that. I didn't know the answer when Leslie asked me this earlier.

I didn't know the answer when Detective Richardson and the other detectives who had taken my statement asked me. All I can do is make a supposition.

"Maybe he was trying to kill Harley and missed. Maybe he wanted to kill Martin as some sort of threat. I have no idea."

Both sound reasonable, but ridiculous at the same time. This is a man who has been obsessed with Harley for years.

Why kill her now?

The kidnapping at least made sense.

"But why would he want her dead?" I ask Leslie who just shakes her head.

"The reason why stalkers are so dangerous is that they do not understand or care about people's boundaries. If you tell a normal person that you do not want them in your life then they accept that and walk away. But a stalker doesn't. And Parker has been given a lot of chances throughout all this time. Mostly by the system."

"What do you mean?" I ask.

"Law enforcement needs to learn to take stalking more seriously. Parker was stalking someone who was originally a stranger who then morphed into this bigger than life person for him. But there are many different types of stalking. Stalking is very common in domestic abuse situations," Leslie explains.

"Like an ex-husband?" Harold asks.

"Everyone jokes about stalking their exes on the internet, and that is one mild form of it. But some people start to take it too far. They follow their exes or their current spouses. They trespass boundaries like taking their phone without their permission. Check up on them all the time. It's a very common thing and it can easily get out of control."

Harold and I nod as we listen.

"So, why do you think this happened?" I ask after a moment. "Why did he kill Martin?"

She doesn't answer at first.

When she finally looks up at me, our eyes meet and I see fear in hers. It takes me aback because I've never seen her this way before. She's not outwardly scared. She isn't shaking.

She is cowering in fear. Her shoulders are straight across, broadened as if in defiance.

But somewhere behind the strong police officer facade there is real fear within her.

"I think it was a threat. He likes to play games and he likes to challenge himself," she says quietly. "I don't think he aimed the gun at Harley at all, I think he aimed his bike at her. And by killing Martin, he wanted to send her a message."

"What kind of message?" Harold asks.

"That he's still around, watching. Lurking. He doesn't want her to forget about him."

When she says that, my body reacts as if its ejected itself from its seat.

I rise up so fast that my knee collides with the table, nearly knocking the coffee cups onto the floor. I walk out into the hallway for some air and space.

Luckily, the foyer out front is vacant and I have some space to meander. I clench my jaw and ball up my fists until they physically hurt.

When will there be the end of this?

How much more must she endure?

The initial faith that I had in the police department and the FBI is all but gone. They are either useless or just don't give a shit.

No, it's time to take this into my own hands. I will forever blame myself for letting this happen to my child but I will not allow anything more to happen to my wife.

The word wife stops me mid-step.

Of course, she's not my wife. She's barely my girlfriend, and yet there doesn't seem to be a more appropriate word for how I feel about her.

One day she will be my wife, but until that happens, she will be safe. I will make sure of it.

"Jackson!" Harold calls my name, walking up to me. "Look what they're saying online."

He hands me his phone and I read the headline and skim the article that follows. Isolated phrases jump out at me.

RECLUSE BILLIONAIRE *of New York's bodyguard shot in the head*

JACKSON LUDLOW LOSES **unborn child in attack**

. . .

*MINETTA FOUNDER'S bodyguard and unborn child killed
by bicycle messenger assassin*

WHEN I LOOK AWAY from the phone, Harley's
parents stand before me looking for an
explanation.

I open my mouth but no words come out.

"What do they mean by unborn child?" Harold
asks quietly, taking the phone away from me.

I could lie.

I could tell them that they are mistaken.

That the papers often get stuff wrong. But to
what end? What would be the point?

Harley didn't tell them about the baby yet, but
she probably would at some point.

"Harley was pregnant," I say slowly, feeling the
weight of each word in my mouth.

"Why didn't you...tell us?" Leslie asks.

"I didn't know for a while. I had a business
thing going on and it put Harley in danger so I
thought it would be best if we took a break."

It's hard to know where to begin and end with
what happened right before I found out about the
pregnancy but I decide to include as much as
possible.

"Then she found out that she was pregnant and
because we were apart, I didn't know."

"Why didn't she tell us?" Leslie turns to Harold.

"She was just trying to figure out what to do. It was still really early. She was all alone."

"So, what happened then?"

I decide to gloss over the whole sneaking into her apartment part and acting like the ex-boyfriend stalker who doesn't know how to respect boundaries.

"She took me back and we were looking forward to having this baby and starting our family."

Leslie starts to cry, collapsing into Harold's arms. I take a few steps back to give them some space.

Their grief overwhelms the room and I know that we are not going to talk anymore for a while.

Without saying another word, I turn around and walk away.

When I order Harley's tea from the barista, I dread going back up to her room and telling her about what just happened.

This was her story to tell, not mine and not the papers'.

8

HARLEY

WHEN I'M ALONE...

B eing alone in the dark isn't as comforting as I thought that it would be. When my parents and Jackson were all cramped into this tiny room, their energy suffocated me.

But now that they are gone, it is my energy that makes it difficult to breathe. In the darkness, the thoughts of everything that I lost are more real.

There is nothing holding them back from flooding my mind.

There is nothing pushing them away. There is nothing giving me perspective about what the future might be other than utter despair.

I use the remote on my bed to turn on the small light above me. It's a reading light that puts out the luminescence of a candle - comforting and cozy.

I sit up a bit in bed and pick up my phone. I

don't bother with news or emails or anything overstimulating.

I need something to take my mind out of this room. I click on the Kindle app and scroll through numerous books, all in various stages of read through. Some I've only gotten through ten percent, but others I've read through completely. None of them seem that appealing at this moment.

Most are uplifting and full of joy, which is not something I want to read right now. Right now I want to read about pain and hate.

The kind of story that I yearn for is one with a happy ending but also with plenty of drama and obstacles for the characters to overcome.

If they don't fight to be together, if they don't endure the worst that life throws at them, what's the fucking point?

I don't see what I want in my library, so I go to Facebook.

Scrolling through my feed, I see books by authors I don't know.

One ad in particular draws my attention and I click on the book and buy it immediately.

The writer has me from the first page and I quickly lose myself in the story.

The wonderful thing about reading is that it allows you to escape. It's a lot like writing, but writing is harder.

You make up the characters and the words and sometimes you get stuck, unsure of where to take the people next.

It's not really the same with reading. A good book grabs you by the hand, pulls you in, and doesn't let you go.

You think about it all the time until you finish it.

And even then, you often want to go back right away and read it all over again. I know. I'm one of those obsessive readers that I am now trying to write for.

With each page that I click through, the darkness that I felt starts to subside.

It's not that I don't feel the pain so much, it's just that the pain is getting overridden by other thoughts.

Instead of losing myself down a rabbit hole of my own emotions and regrets, I suddenly have something else to think about. And that's enough for now.

A KNOCK on the door startles me, pulling me away from my phone and forcing me into reality.

"Come in," I say. Luckily, it's Jackson and not my parents.

It's not that I don't want to see them, it's just that the fact that I haven't told them about the pregnancy is weighing on me.

It's a secret that I have to tell but it's also one that I don't feel like I have the strength to reveal right now.

"Thanks for the tea. Took you long enough," I say, jokingly.

"I ran into your parents downstairs and we talked for a bit."

"I'm glad."

"So...how are you?"

I shrug. There's no way to really answer that question and I know that he knows that.

"Just trying to think about something else, you know?" I gesture to the phone.

"Yes, I do."

I take a sip of the mint green tea and savor the feeling of its warmth in my mouth.

He doesn't say anything for a bit and just stares into space somewhere above me.

That's when I suddenly realize that it wasn't just me who lost the baby. I've known this before, of course, but not really known it.

I didn't know it in my bone marrow, at the very center of my being.

"I am sorry," I whisper. Jackson looks at me, surprised. "I am sorry for your loss."

I reach my arms up to him and he glides into them. I wrap my arms around him and we hold each other for a while.

Tears start to flow and I hear his thick sobs echoing against my body.

He was there for me when I needed space and darkness and now, I'm here for him when he needs comfort.

He lifts his legs up onto the bed and I move over to make some room. Minutes tick by and we stay there, pressing our bodies against each other's.

We mourn our child and the future as it could've been.

A loud knock startles both of us. Before we can say 'come in,' the door swings open and my parents come in.

"Oh, sorry," my dad says quickly.

"It's fine," Jackson says, climbing off me. My mom flips on the big light, and I shield my eyes.

"Um, Harley—" Jackson starts to say. I look over at him, he looks scared. His eyes won't meet mine. I can tell that he's hiding something.

"Yeah?"

"I should've told you right away, but everything has been happening so fast."

I wait for him to continue.

9

HARLEY

WHEN THEY KNOW...

"I'm so sorry, honey." Mom rushes over to me, wrapping her arms around me.

"About what?" I ask.

My dad comes over, patting my head.

Then it hits me.

Jackson told them.

I thought that I would be upset by this, but my reaction in that moment is just relief. It's something that has been weighing on me ever since they first got here. It's something I should've told them but I couldn't quite find the words.

No, that's not true. I knew that if I were to say those words out loud - I was pregnant. I lost the baby - then I would've probably lost myself as well.

And now, Jackson gave me the biggest gift he could have.

He told them himself.

"I'm so sorry that they found out this way, Harley," Jackson says over and over again somewhere in the distance.

He's standing right next to us, but it doesn't feel like he's here at all. It's as if he's talking through plexiglass.

I want to answer him.

I want to tell him that it's alright, I forgive him. That there's actually nothing to forgive, but I can't. Not until my parents pull away.

Eventually, they do.

I dry my tears and try to compose myself.

In order to do that, I can't think about what happened and what I lost, what *we* lost. I just have to think past it, if that makes any sense.

"I'm really sorry, Harley," Jackson says again.

"It's fine, really. I'm just glad that you know."

I expect my parents to come at me with a million questions about why I didn't tell them earlier, but they take me by surprise. Instead, they just tell me how sorry they are over everything that I've been through and that they love me.

AFTER SUCH AN OUTPOURING OF EMOTION, **we are all**

spent and exhausted and spend the next few hours talking about anything but the baby.

My mom focuses the conversation on the task at hand; finding Parker and holding him accountable for everything that he has done.

She is convinced that it was him who was on the bike, but I am not so sure. I know that he fits the profile and it did look like him physically but Parker was never this daring before.

Whenever he approached me before, he was always so...timid. Unsure of himself.

Then again, when his threats got worse and worse, he did start to put off a completely different vibe.

"I still don't know how the papers could've found out about this so quickly," Jackson says when the conversation reaches somewhat of a lull.

I now know that they actually found out about the death of their unborn grandchild, not from Jackson, but from Page Six, a popular celebrity section of the New York Post.

Other blogs and gossip papers picked up the story, including those owned by Minetta.

"Did you tell anyone at Minetta about what happened?"

Jackson swallows hard and I know the answer before he even says a word.

"Only Phillips and a few other people I thought that I could trust."

"They probably leaked it."

"No, they wouldn't leak it to the Post. They are a competing paper."

I shake my head, shrugging my shoulders.

"What?" he asks.

"They couldn't very well publish it in a blog or a paper that Minetta owns. Not initially. Then you'd know for sure. But if the Post publishes it first, then they can just jump on the bandwagon but publish all the juicy details themselves."

It's as if a lightbulb goes off in his head. His face lights up and then quickly turns to anger and disappointment.

"Honestly, it doesn't really matter, does it?" I ask.

"How can you say that?"

"I just assumed that it would be on the news one way or another. A bike messenger shooting someone in the head in plain sight is still not a normal news day in New York City. And the fact that you are kind of known in the city as a recluse billionaire just added more spice to the story."

"But what about the baby?" he asks. "How did they know that?"

I shrug. That I don't know.

He paces around the room trying to figure it out.

"I didn't tell anyone at Minetta about that. It was our secret. Who else knew besides me?" he asks.

"Martin. Julie. But they kept it quiet. And I don't think Julie has given any statements about anything since it happened. She would never tell anyone anyway."

We go through all the people that we know who could've possibly been the source and no one seems like a good candidate.

If they knew about us and the shooting they didn't know about the baby.

No one really did before Jackson, Julie, and Martin.

And then another name pops into my head.

"What about Aurora?" I ask.

He looks at me surprised.

"How is she?" my mom asks.

She left her husband in Europe and has been staying with Jackson for a bit, I want to say but I bite my tongue.

I don't want to be mean-spirited and I don't want to complain to my parents about something that doesn't concern them.

But the fact that she is there still annoys me.

She has money. She has friends. Why does she have to stay at Jackson's?

"She's a big shareholder in Minetta now," I say.

"Right," Jackson says through his teeth.

"Did she know about the baby?" my dad asks.

"No, she didn't. I haven't seen her in a while. You know that, Harley."

"Well, actually, I don't, but that's what you have said."

Jackson takes a deep breath, letting it out slowly.

"She doesn't know anything about this. It's not Aurora."

"So, who could it be?" I ask. He shrugs. I shrug, too.

We try to go over the names again but we just keep going in circles. Why does it even matter? Someone knew and someone told.

Maybe it's fine that this secret is out.

Maybe it shouldn't have been a secret at all. I take the last sip of my tea and place the cup back on the tray next to the bed.

When I glance up at my mom, she has a concerned look on her face.

"What is it?" I ask.

"What if it was Parker?"

10

HARLEY

Martin's funeral is held a few days later. His company made all the arrangements and Jackson paid for it.

Martin never told me about his family and I am surprised when I see both of his parents and his brothers and sisters along with their spouses and kids filling up the front two rows.

When we first walk into the funeral home for the viewing, Jackson nudges me to go and say something to them, but I'm not ready.

I find a seat closest to the door and stay there.

The service is heartbreaking, and it's all I can do to make it through it. Tears roll down my cheeks without my permission.

There's nothing I can do to make them stop. This man is dead because of me. That's the only thought that runs through my mind over and over again. I know that he was just doing his job.

He was my bodyguard. But were it not for me, he would still be alive.

After the service, I watch Julie kneel over his lifeless body. I still haven't seen it and it's time for me to pay my respects. I want to run screaming out of the building, but Jackson pulls me by my arm to the front.

Martin's family gives Julie some space and time alone with him, but as soon as she pulls away from the casket, they huddle around her, placing her in a protective cocoon.

That's perfectly fine with me. I haven't seen or spoken to her since it happened.

I thought that maybe she would visit me in the hospital, but she didn't. When I did go home, she wasn't there. I tried texting and calling her, but she never answered me.

Julie is dressed in a long black dress and a form-fitting black blazer. Her eyes are bloodshot with dark black bags underneath. She is wearing sunglasses, even though we are all inside, and so is Martin's mom.

"Julie, I'm so sorry," I whisper, walking up to her.

I open my arms to bring her in for a hug, but she just walks past me. Her rebuke startles me.

I have no idea why she did that. Is she angry with me?

I'm about to go after her, but instead Jackson leads me to the casket and forces me to look at Martin.

They did their best to cover up the bullet hole in his forehead, in fact, it's hard to even see it at all if you don't know what you're looking for.

But looking at him now, it's all I see. I blink and I'm back on that pavement staring into his open lifeless eyes.

My body starts to shake and I feel like I'm going to throw up.

Before I make a scene, I break free from Jackson's ironclad grasp on my arm and run out of the room.

I FIND Julie in the bathroom, standing in front of the mirror, applying concealer under her eyes.

At first, I ignore her when I walk into one of the stalls, but I quickly walk straight back out.

"I'm so sorry for your loss, Julie. You know that, right?" I ask, walking right next to her.

"And I am sorry for yours," she says coldly.

We stand staring at each other for a few moments. I don't understand why she's so angry with me. I search her face, but I can't find the answer.

I turn on the sink and splash some water on my face. It feels cool and refreshing, but only for a moment.

"I'm not sure what else to say," I confess. "I'm just so sorry."

I try to hug her again, but this time she physically pushes me away.

"Harley, I can't, okay?"

"Why? What's wrong?"

"Are you serious?"

I stare at her.

"Are you seriously asking me what's wrong at my boyfriend's funeral? After he got murdered right in front of me?"

Well, technically in front of me, I correct her silently.

"No, and you know that," I say. "I'm trying to hug you and give you my condolences and you're just refusing to even talk to me."

She shakes her head. Suddenly, the stern facade disappears and a waterfall of tears starts to fall down her face. I reach for her again, but again she pulls away.

"Get away from me," she says. "I don't want you to touch me."

"Why?" I start to cry along with her. "You're my best friend. I'm so sorry. I want to be here for you."

"Well, you can't," she barks back.

"Why?" I plead with her.

"Don't you get it, Harley? Don't you *fucking* get it?"

I stare at her, not entirely sure what she means.

"Martin is dead because of you."

Her words hit me like a punch to the face. I hate her for saying it. I hate her for confirming what I already believe. She shouldn't blame me. She should let me be here for her. But when I look back at her, all I see is rage.

"Julie, we both lost him. He became a good friend of mine throughout this whole thing. I miss him, too, but that doesn't mean —"

She cuts me off by putting her hand over my mouth.

"Shut up," she whispers. I have never seen her like this before. Usually, she yells and screams or cries. But now she is calm and it terrifies me.

Instead of pushing away her hand, I take a step back and wait for her to let it fall back to her side.

"We both lost people, Julie," I say quietly. "You lost your boyfriend. I lost my..." My words trail off. I can't even say it out loud at first. "I lost my baby."

"No," she says, shaking her head. "You didn't lose

your baby. You weren't even sure if you wanted to keep it a few weeks ago. So don't act like you lost anything as big as what I lost. I didn't just lose my boyfriend, Harley, I lost my best friend. My future husband. The father of my future children. I lost *everything*."

11

HARLEY

WHEN THERE'S MORE PAIN....

I nod and take another step back.

If you start to play the game of comparisons in terms of whose life is worse or who suffered more, you will both lose in the end.

Her words hurt me to my core, but I can see, perhaps a little too late, that this is not the time to talk to her about anything.

I should walk away. I shouldn't talk to her now. I know this, but still, something makes me try again.

"I'm not trying to compare your loss to my loss, Julie, I'm just trying to make you understand," I say.

"Understand what?"

"That I'm sorry for your loss. I am sorry that Martin's gone."

"Well, thank you *very* much! I mean, where would I be without your condolences, Harley?" Julie says sarcastically.

"Okay, I'm going to go," I say, walking past her. But she puts out her hand to block me.

"He's dead because of you," she whispers into my ear. "Do you know what that means? Do you know how that makes me feel?"

"You and I both know that he's dead because of Parker. I didn't kill him, Julie. He was a bodyguard. He protected me."

"Well, he should've protected himself."

"Yeah, maybe you're right. Maybe he should've. But he didn't."

"I'm just so angry, Harley. I'm so angry over everything." Tears start to roll down her face. I pull her close to me, and this time I don't let go. She cries into my shoulder and my whole body shakes with her sobs.

"I can't...I can't." She pushes me away, wrapping her arms around herself. "You should've died at that cabin, Harley. Then Martin would still be alive."

She says that and walks away. I don't follow her. I'm in too much pain. I bend in half and collapse onto the floor. Her words have cut me as if they were a knife. I knew that she would be angry and upset but I didn't know that she could be that cruel.

———————

I DON'T KNOW how long I sit on the floor of that bathroom, but sometime later, Jackson comes in and physically lifts me up.

"I knew that I shouldn't have come here," I mumble over and over again as I try to explain to him what has just happened between Julie and me.

"She's just upset. She didn't mean it," he says. "I'm sure that after some time passes, everything will be fine."

Maybe he's right. At least, maybe on her end. But I'm not sure how long it will take me to forget what she has said to me. I'm not sure one lifetime is enough time.

———————

I DON'T WANT to go home again, but there are some things that I need to get.

I decide to go to Jackson's without even asking him for an invitation. I am glad that one is not required.

He just drives me to my apartment and helps me pack two suitcases of things.

I take everything that I think I will need, including old journals, my computer, and all of my favorite clothes.

The apartment seems empty without Martin and Julie whispering in the kitchen and I can't wait to get out of there.

"It wasn't that long ago when he was here all the time," I say, zipping up the bigger suitcase. "It's just so weird being here without him."

"Yeah, I know," Jackson says even though there's no way he could know.

Martin wasn't here that long, but the space is small and he quickly became a part of things without even trying.

No, that's not true.

Martin was a great addition to our little home.

He put Julie at ease and created a buffer between us that I didn't even know we needed. I always thought we got along, but it wasn't until he was here that I realized how well we could get along.

"Thanks for coming to my place," Jackson says in the car after we pull away from my street.

"No, thank you for letting me come over even without an invitation," I say, staring out of the window at the shiny lights whizzing past us.

"I've been meaning to ask you this for a while

now, so I guess this is as good a time as any," Jacksons says after a moment.

"What?" I ask, without turning to look at him.

"What if you don't just come to stay with me?"

I look at him, not sure where he's going with that.

"What if you move in with me instead?"

I give him a brief nod even before I can fully process the question.

"What is that?" he asks. "Is that a yes?"

"Yes, that's a yes," I say quietly.

He puts his hand on mine, giving it a little squeeze.

We ride the rest of the way in silence. My thoughts return to Julie and the things that she said to me at the funeral.

This is not exactly how I wanted things to end. In fact, I hope it's not the end. But it is for now.

She doesn't want me in her life.

She blames me for her boyfriend's death. I've tried to make amends, but what else can I do?

We pull up to his house around back and he presses the button to open the garage door that is completely hidden from sight.

"Just give it some time," Jackson says, as if he can read my mind.

I nod.

"Welcome home."

12

HARLEY

WHEN I LOOK AROUND MY NEW HOME....

I wake up the following morning in Jackson's big bed all alone.

Nothing happened the night before except me climbing under the covers and falling asleep.

The funeral has drained me of the little energy I had left, leaving me completely spent.

This morning, even though I slept more than twelve hours, I don't feel any more rested than I did the night before.

I take a shower, wrap my hair in a towel, and put back on what I wore last night: my favorite pair of loose and tropical colored pajama pants along with a soft gray sweater.

I'd hate to admit this to anyone out loud, but I often wear the same thing to bed as I do around the house, especially on the days that I don't leave home. And not every day feels like a leggings day.

Some days, you want to be even more comfortable than that.

By the time I get downstairs, I'm regretting that I did not bring my laptop, my journal, or my phone.

I had forgotten how big this house is.

Unlike my apartment, where I could see all around it just by looking up from my bed, this place almost requires a map.

By now, I know pretty much where everything is but it doesn't change the fact that it still takes at least five minutes to walk from the master bedroom upstairs all the way down to the kitchen at the opposite end of the house.

When I took off on my journey, I was expecting to see Jackson somewhere upstairs working in another room, to give me the quiet to sleep in. But much to my surprise, he is nowhere to be found.

The house is all mine and it's quite disarming.

"So, this is where I live now?" I say out loud, making my way back from the kitchen and toward the staircase.

I run my fingers over the railing and admire its smooth wood and the workmanship that went into making this what it is.

Who were the men who carved this wood? Who were the men who cut down the trees?

Never in a million years did I ever imagine living in a place like this.

I am living here, yes, but am I really living here as an equal partner?

As I head upstairs to get my laptop and phone, I wonder about that. It's not like I can afford to pay half the mortgage on this place.

Does he even have a mortgage?

So, what does it really mean that I live here?

With Julie, I had to pay half the rent no matter what.

And so did she. When she moved out with Logan, she still owed me the rent until I found another roommate to cover for her. But here? In this place, I will always be a stranger.

Walking back down the stairs, something else occurs to me. I am not the only stranger here.

This place doesn't feel like Jackson at all. Maybe when I first met him, this place fit who he was.

But now?

I don't know, something just does not feel right. It's almost like we are both living here only temporarily.

After pouring myself a cup of tea, I sit down at the kitchen island and pick up my phone.

I see a text from Jackson that says that he had to go in to the office and will be back later.

Another unread text is from my mom.

My parents have been back in Montana for a few days and she's just texting to see how I'm feeling about everything. I send her a thumbs up emoji and promise to call later this afternoon.

A part of me wishes that they were still here, and another part is glad that they're back home.

As much as I enjoy spending time with them, I always feel like I have to be on my best behavior around them.

Especially around my mom.

If I look too tired, or act even a little bit too emotional, she immediately becomes concerned. I don't know if it's just a mom thing or her personality in particular, but for some reason I feel this pressure to be perfect around her.

It's like I don't want her to worry, so I have to pretend that everything is fine. Otherwise, she instantaneously assumes that the worst is going to happen.

Briefly, I glance at the number of unanswered emails that are piling up in my inbox and decide that nothing's going to happen if I let them go for another few hours.

Instead, I click on the Kindle app and return to my book.

The put-upon wealthy guy who doesn't want the pressures of his wealth is about to make his father very angry and I can't wait to find out what happens next.

"Oh, hello." A familiar voice startles me.

There was no ring of the doorbell, no sound of shoes on the parquet floors. She just appears, as if out of thin air.

"Hello," I say. She walks over to me, her sandy blond hair bouncing with each step. It takes me a moment to realize that she's walking toward me to give me a hug, and I turn in my chair at the last second to hug her back.

"It's nice to see you again, Harley. I am so sorry about everything that happened."

"Thank you." I nod. "I really appreciate that."

She walks over to the refrigerator and looks inside. It's empty, holding only a lonely packet of Brussels sprouts in the bottom drawer.

"When was the last time Jackson had food in here?" she asks. "I guess I'll be ordering out."

While everyone wants visitors to be comfortable in their homes, she's definitely crossing boundaries by acting as if this were *her* home.

"I'm sorry, I don't mean to be rude," I finally say. "But what you are doing here, Aurora?"

13

HARLEY

WHEN WE PLAY GAMES....

Aurora walks around the kitchen as if it were her own.

Suddenly, I don't feel like the girlfriend of the owner but the help.

She pauses to look out of the window before answering.

I don't know if Jackson has invited her or not and I don't feel comfortable asking her to leave.

But her presence makes me uneasy. She doesn't answer my question and I don't bother asking it again. Instead, I just grab my laptop and my phone and head out of the room.

"Where are you going?" she asks.

I pause in the hallway in between the kitchen and the formal dining room.

"You weren't saying anything, so I figure that

you didn't come here to talk," I say these words without turning around. Then I continue to walk away.

"Listen, I'm sorry." Aurora catches up to me. "I didn't mean to make you feel uncomfortable."

Now that we are actually eye-to-eye, I can see that she really means this. But why else would she act this way? Like I'm invisible. Oh, yeah, maybe in her eyes I was.

"So, what are you doing here?" I ask, exhaling quickly.

She moves her jaw from one side of her head to another, as if to stretch it. Then she purses her lips and relaxes them slowly.

"I just didn't know where else to go."

I nod, resisting the temptation to roll my eyes. This is the place that Aurora runs to whenever her life gets a little bit difficult.

It doesn't sound like she lives a particularly easy life, but it does seem like she craves the drama.

Perhaps, she does it because she always has this place to come back to. Jackson is her soft place to fall.

"I know that I shouldn't be barging in on you both. Maybe it's not the right thing to do."

Maybe? I want to say, but I bite my tongue.

She turns back around and walks back to the kitchen. Does she expect me to just follow?

Does she expect me to put my whole day on hold just because she is here? What annoys me the most is the way that she just expects help to come about whenever she's here.

She shows up and Jackson is just supposed to drop everything and deal with her problem.

Well, Jackson is not here and I'm not him.

Since she walked away from me expecting me to follow, I pretend that I don't know what she wants.

I don't know if she's actually that dense or just wants to play games, but either way, I'm the one who lives here.

If she wants to talk to me then she'll have to be the one to ask.

I turn around and walk toward the stairs.

"Wait, Harley! Where are you going?"

I walk halfway up the stairs, requiring her to call my name a couple more times before I respond.

"You just walked away, so I figured I'd get back to what I was doing."

I look down at her from the staircase. She looks small and timid and not at all as intimidating as she is face to face.

"I'm sorry..." she says slowly. "I just thought that you would...follow me."

She says the last bit very quietly and slowly. I can see her expectation of me finally dawning on her.

Why was she expecting me to follow her?

Just because everyone else does? Well, just because everyone else in her life makes accommodations for her doesn't mean that I am about to.

Then something dawns on me. Maybe I just need to come right out and say what I want her to do.

"Aurora, Jackson is not here. If you want to talk to me then you have to ask me. Otherwise, I'm just going to go back to my day."

My directness takes her by surprise, but then a look of relief comes over her.

"Yes, please. I need to talk to you."

I nod, hovering my foot over the step below me.

"Can we have some coffee?"

"Sure, but I'd prefer a cup of tea."

AURORA SITS down at the kitchen island and I put on the kettle. She opts for tea as well, and I place two bags in two white mugs. I watch the water start to boil in the electric glass kettle and wait for her to start.

"I'm sorry for barging in on you like that. I've just always thought of this place as my own."

Thanks for that, Jackson, I say to myself sarcastically. But I appreciate the apology.

"It's okay. I understand. But I also want you to know that I'm living here now. Full-time."

"Really?"

"Yeah, Jackson asked me to move in with him."

"That's great. I'm really happy for you," she says. She isn't just saying that to be nice, I can tell that she's being earnest and I appreciate that.

"I also wanted to say that I heard about what happened to you."

My whole body tightens up. I clench my jaw and brace myself against the marble.

"I read that you were pregnant."

I swallow hard. My mouth goes dry and when I open it to speak, a cough comes out.

"Yeah..."

It's all I manage to say.

"I'm sorry, I shouldn't have brought it up. I just wanted you to know that I know."

"I appreciate that."

What I appreciate more is her saying that I don't have to talk to her about it.

"So, what's going on with you?"

"I don't know if you know but I moved in with Elliot Woodward."

The asshole who attacked me? I want to ask, but I fight the urge.

"I think Jackson mentioned that you were...together."

"Yeah, well, not anymore."

"What happened?"

"With the whole #metoo movement, a lot of women have been coming forward and saying all this stuff about how he came onto them.

"Anyway, a few who work for him have filed a lawsuit. He got really pissed and we got into this fight."

I listen and don't really know what to say. I guess I should try to comfort her, but the truth is that no matter how much I don't really like her, she doesn't deserve to be with a degenerate like that.

"So, what do you think about what those women are saying?" I ask, instead of coming straight out and stating my opinion.

"I don't know what to think. I mean, there are a lot of them. But he never really did anything to me."

I shake my head.

"What?" she asks, catching me in my disgust.

"Aurora, he probably did all of that they're accusing him of."

"How do you know?"

"Because he kissed me, forcefully. And when I tried to push him away, he wouldn't take no for answer."

"What?" Aurora asks, horrified.

"Yeah, so I had to bite down on his lips to get him to stop."

"No, I can't believe it," she says, shaking her head.

14
_____

HARLEY

WHEN WE TALK....

Her reaction makes me angry. There's no way I can prove it to her, but why the hell would I make up something like this?

It's embarrassing and demeaning. I want nothing more than to not have had this happen.

"I'm sorry, I didn't mean it that way," Aurora says.

"What did you fight about?" I ask, trying to pivot the conversation in another direction.

"Well, sort of about that. I mean, I just couldn't believe that all of those women are lying and he didn't like that."

"That's because they aren't," I say under my breath.

"So, what did he do to you?" she asks quietly.

I tell her exactly what happened, every last

detail. I don't elaborate and I don't use flowery language to make a point. I just state the facts. At the end, she gasps.

"That's so...shitty."

"Yeah, it was. If I hadn't bitten him, he wouldn't have stopped."

She nods, burying her head in her hands.

"Why does this always happen? Why am I always attracted to these assholes?" she asks through her sobs.

I don't really know how to answer that, or that she wants me to answer it at all. She just wants someone to listen, and I do. I put my arm around her and listen to her cry.

"You deserve someone a lot better than Elliot Woodward. I hope you know that."

"That's what Jackson told me as well."

"Well, he's right."

"I just don't know where to find a good guy, you know?"

I shrug. "Maybe you should start with just not looking at all. I mean, Jackson said that you don't stay by yourself for long."

I don't really know Aurora, so telling her to stop dating altogether feels like it's not entirely my place. Yet, I can't help myself.

"My husband has been begging me to take him back," she mumbles through the tears.

"Didn't he hit you?" I ask.

She shrugs. "Sometimes."

"Don't you care?"

She shrugs again and says, "Sometimes."

"Well, you should. You don't deserve to be treated like that. No one does. There are good men out there. And they won't hit you and they won't make you feel like you're nothing."

"Yeah, but do they have money?"

I stare at her in disbelief. Is she really saying these words?

"You are already rich," I say. "You don't need to date anyone for money."

"Eh, I'm not that rich."

I shake my head.

Being in the presence of the few wealthy people I've met since getting involved with Jackson, I realized that this is a notion that only the wealthy have.

Poor people, and by that, I mean everyone who isn't in the 1%, tends to think that there's a certain amount of money that will make them comfortable and then they will have enough.

But the 1% are different.

Most of them think that whatever they have isn't enough and it's never going to be enough.

"Aurora, you are rich. And even if you weren't, you do not need to date a man for his wealth.

There are a lot better characteristics by which to judge someone than their bank account."

She looks at me as if I have lost my mind.

"You are one to talk," she says, smiling.

"I am not dating Jackson for his money. I am dating him in spite of it. I mean, some money is good, of course. I had a lot of problems paying my bills but beyond that? I don't need much beyond that."

Suddenly, she starts to laugh. Aurora throws her head back and her whole body starts to shake.

"What's so funny?"

"Don't you get it?" she asks. "That's the whole thing. I can't pay my fucking bills either."

I stare at her, dumbfounded.

"My estranged husband has cut me off. Most of my credit cards are frozen. Elliot was helping me out, but now that we had this fight, he kicked me out and took all the money that he put into an account for me."

"Don't you have any of your own money?"

"Yeah, I did. Some. But I wrote Jackson a pretty big check. And most of it is joint property with my husband. So, it's all tied up in litigation."

I don't know what to say. I never thought that a person who could write a two million dollar check would have a problem with money at all. But here she is, sitting in Jackson's house, waiting for him to get home so that he can help her out financially.

"What about getting a job?" I ask, after a moment.

"What?" She looks at me like I have lost my mind.

"Yeah, I know, it's a radical idea. But you could get a job."

"And what would this job pay? Seventy, eighty-thousand a year?"

Now, it's my turn to laugh.

"You would be extremely lucky to get a position that paid that much," I say. "It would be more like thirty. Thirty-five. I'm not entirely sure what you are qualified to do."

"So, what would be the point of that?" Aurora asks.

"To make your own way in life. To live just on what you make. It's not such a terrible thing. It's actually quite liberating."

15

HARLEY

DIFFERENCES OF OPINION....

I t's hard for me to understand Aurora just like it's probably hard for her to understand me.

She has lived in the lap of luxury for a very long time, so long indeed that it has made her fearful of what life would be like without money.

Yes, it can be difficult and challenging to be poor, but the truth is that it's also incredibly liberating.

Even if you don't make much, just the ability to pay for all of your bills entirely using your own wits and time, well, there's nothing quite like it.

It gives you this sense of freedom and possibility. You don't owe anyone anything.

You may not like your job or your boss but just the very fact that you get a paycheck at the end and it's all yours…it's hard to explain what it feels like to someone who never had that before.

"You don't understand where I'm coming from yet, but you will soon enough," Aurora says.

"What do you mean?"

"You've only just moved in with Jackson. He has more money than most people can even dream of."

"Yeah, so?"

"There's no way that you'll be able to go back to busting your butt at a job you hate for a measly forty-thousand dollars a year."

"You don't think so?" I ask, challenging her.

"I know so."

I shake my head, refusing to believe her.

"How can you be so sure?"

She narrows her eyes and brings her face really close to mine.

"Harley, you don't even know what it's like to have the kind of money that he does. People whose spouses make two-hundred thousand a year don't work for money. And his net worth is probably half a billion, even after he lost all that money to that fraudster."

I hate to admit it, but this is something that has crossed my mind before.

I've never depended on a man before I met Jackson, and it's still a big concern of mine going forward.

He has so much money that it makes whatever I could possibly make at a real job not noticeable at all.

So, it's easy to say, why not just not work? But what's going to happen in a year or two, or after a decade or more?

Do I go through my life just relying on money that's not mine?

"I know what you're thinking," she says, with a little smile at the corner of her lips.

I wait for her to continue.

"His money is his now, but it won't be after a while. If you stay together, it will be like any other relationship. What's his becomes yours and what's yours becomes his."

"That's...hard to imagine," I admit.

"You won't even notice it after a little bit. I mean, yeah, at first you'll be impressed by the private plane and all the places that you can go and all the five-star accommodations, but after a bit, it will be something you expect. And that's when it will be difficult to give up."

I shake my head. No, that won't happen to me, I promise myself.

"I thought that it wouldn't happen to me either. But here I am, putting up with a terrible ex just because I'm afraid of losing what we have together."

"You still deserve better than him and Elliot. No man should hit a woman."

She nods her head. I know that she knows but it doesn't feel like she knows it deep in her heart.

Neither of us says anything for a few moments and then Aurora excuses herself, disappearing into the bathroom.

I run my fingertips over the smooth marble surface and look around the room, wondering if this place will ever feel like home. Maybe Aurora is right. Maybe I don't know what I'm talking about.

Perhaps, one day all of this will just be too much to give up.

But the more I look around the room, the less enamored I get with everything that I see around me.

Why would anything in this kitchen matter to me at all? It's just stuff. They're just things.

They're nice, of course, but who really cares?

While I wait for her to return, I open my laptop and read my emails for the first time since it all happened.

The third book in my series has released and the emails that have come in from readers who have pre-ordered it and bought it soon after it went live take me aback. If I were standing, then they'd bring me to my knees.

My whole body starts to shake as I read their kind words of congratulations and praise.

Just the thought that someone would take time out of their day to write to someone who they don't know and tell them how much a book means to them takes me by surprise.

This isn't the first time I've received an email like this, but the fact that people actually keep writing me just takes my breath away.

I've really enjoyed books in the past. I've read some over and over again, and yet, to look up the author's email or to look them up on social media and send a message somehow never occurred to me.

I mean, why would they want to hear from me? They probably have a ton of fans.

But now that I am on the other end of that, things feel different.

I am grateful for each and every message that I receive because it gives what I am doing newfound meaning.

Suddenly, it's all starting to make sense.

16

HARLEY

WHAT THIS MEANS TO ME...

E ven though, growing up, I never really thought it would be possible to make money writing, somehow now that it's actually happening, it is.

And now that I'm doing it, I realize that there's a whole other dimension to the sales as well.

Yes, I receive about $2.74 for each book that I sell, but that money represents so much more.

That two dollars and almost seventy-five cents is also the person reading something that I have written.

Time is a precious commodity and yet these people are taking time out of their day to spend it with my books.

I carefully read each email and write back a

response. It's never one word, but it is occasionally just the phrase "thank you."

But the more that the person writes to me, the more that she shares with me, the more I share back. It's the least I can do.

As I write back each and every person who took the time to write me, I wonder what it is about my books that's really striking a chord with them?

I mean, I know what I'm trying to do with my writing.

There are writers out there that want to make their sentences as fancy and highfalutin' as possible. I don't know why they strive for that except I suspect that they want to just show off the fact that they may own a thesaurus.

I'm not like that.

To me, the point of language is to communicate and I want my books to be written as simply and directly as possible.

And that mainly means to write just as I speak and think.

In the last email that I read, a woman named Judy says:

I'M NOT sure if you will ever read this, but I want you to know that your writing helped me through a very dark part of my life. My husband is in and out of the hospital and I spend a lot of my time sitting by his bedside while he sleeps. That means that I spend a lot of my time reading your books on my phone. What I like best about them is how easy they are to read. No matter what I just went through, I can always pick up at seemingly any paragraph and just start and they take me away from my troubles. I can't wait to read more! Keep them coming!

I READ the email over and over again, choking back tears.

I've never felt this way about a writer, and I never in my life thought that anyone would feel like that about my own work.

Suddenly, I feel the full weight of responsibility on my shoulders and it gives me a newfound purpose.

What I am doing here with my writing is not just a passing fancy. I am not just indulging myself and wasting time.

No, it's important.

I am helping people escape.

I am helping to distract people from the pressures of everyday life. If my words take a person in a difficult situation and help them through it just a little bit, well, that's...everything. That's all I can ever ask for.

It takes me a while to go through all the emails and write every single person back. I save Judy's email for last and I send off my reply just as Aurora comes back into the room.

"What were you working on so hard?" she asks.

"Just writing back some of my readers."

She looks at me with a confused expression on her face.

That's when it occurs to me that she doesn't really know what I do. I debate for a moment whether or not I should keep my line of work to myself, but then I decide against it.

I've kept my writing a secret for long enough, and it's about time that I start putting myself out there.

"I'm actually a writer. An author. So, I was writing back some of my fans."

"Wait, what? You're an author?"

I nod.

"What's the difference between the two again?"

"Well, people who write can just be writers, meaning that all they do is write. But some of them are also authors, meaning that they do all the publishing and marketing themselves. You know all that stuff that goes into making the book available to the public."

"So, what kind of stories do you write?" Aurora asks. "And why hasn't Jackson told me about this?"

"I always wanted to be a writer, but it wasn't until I met Jackson and he inspired me to just go ahead and put my writing out there, publish it myself, that anything happened."

"What do you mean?"

"Well, before him, I was always submitting short stories and things like that to literary magazines and publishers. I submitted a chapter outline and query letter about a young adult novel to a million different agents, but never really heard back anything. And then Jackson came along. And he was like, 'why don't you just self-publish your stuff and see what happens?' Well, not exactly like that. If I had just self-published, nothing probably would've happened."

"So what did you do?"

"I learned a lot about digital marketing and Facebook advertising and building a brand. So, that all went into becoming an author."

"That's so awesome," Aurora says, nodding her head. She seems really interested so I continue.

"I write novels. Romance novels but not really traditional romance novels. There's one love story that goes through the whole thing but there's also a lot of suspense and thriller elements to it."

I don't go so far as to mention that I basically

write from real life because I'm not quite ready to share everything with Aurora quite yet.

"With sex?" Aurora asks, her eyes lighting up.

17

HARLEY

WHEN I TELL HER...

I shrug, not sure how to answer her question.

"Oh my God! I have to read your books!"

"Do you like those kind of books?"

"Of course! Who doesn't?"

"You'd be surprised," I say, shrugging my shoulders.

"What do you mean?"

"Well, when you look on Amazon and other retail sites, these types of book are so popular. And I think it's awesome. I mean, they are really empowering to women. They have strong women characters and they're about love conquering anything in life. And they're all mainly written by women, making them extra special, you know?"

I can tell by the expression on her face that she doesn't quite know what I'm getting at.

"Well, most of the authors are women and a huge majority of them are self-published. They are mothers and wives and this is what they do for a living. And some of them make a ton of money. So, it's just really awesome for me to be involved in an industry that's fueled by women and supported by women and created for women."

"Yeah, that is pretty unique, huh?" Aurora nods her head. "So, do you have a lot of sales?"

"I have sales, which is pretty awesome," I admit. "I don't think you'd say I have a lot of sales, but I am really happy with the results. I'd like to sell even more books in the future though, don't get me wrong."

I laugh and then she laughs along with me. When she asks me for the names of my books, I tell her and she quickly puts them into her phone.

"Oh my God! There you are! I can't believe it."

I shrug my shoulders. This is the first time that anyone actually looked up my books right in front of me and I blush a bit.

"One-click. One-click. One-click!" she says excitedly.

I blush even more.

"Don't be embarrassed," Aurora adds, nudging me with her shoulder. But I can't help but shy away from her.

"Okay, but I have to warn you, the books are a bit...explicit."

"You mean dirty?"

I nod.

"Don't worry about me. I like my books really dirty. The dirtier the better."

I take a deep breath and let it out slowly. God help me. Is this really happening? Is Jackson's ex-wife really going to read my books?

To calm my nerves, I walk over to the faucet and pour myself a glass of water. It feels cold and smooth against the back of my throat and I relish the moment.

"So, what about you?" I ask, finishing the glass and pouring myself another. "Was there anything you ever wanted to do since you were a little girl?"

"Um..." she says, without taking her eyes off her phone. I assume that she's texting someone, so I wait. But instead of typing anything, she just scrolls down with her thumb.

"What are you doing?" I ask. She doesn't reply. Instead, she just keeps reading.

I walk over and grab the phone out of her hand.

"Hey!" she yells as I look at the screen. She's at the end of the first chapter of my first book.

"You're reading my book?"

"You said I could."

"I didn't mean *now*. In front of me!"

"Why not?" She looks at me, innocently.

"Because...because...."

I don't know how to answer her. There isn't really a good answer. I'm just suddenly so overwhelmed by the prospect of her reading about my life.

While it can be a lot easier to just write exactly what has happened to you instead of making things up, when someone you know reads the words and knows the truth, everything suddenly becomes so much more complicated.

"You're good," Aurora says, taking her phone out of my hand.

"Thank you. But that doesn't mean that you can read this book right now."

"Okay, fine," she says, putting the phone on the counter. "I won't. I promise."

I feel satisfied, but I know that this feeling is fleeting.

I see the way that she's looking at me, with this newfound curiosity.

My throat closes up and my hands get clammy.

In a few hours, Aurora is going to know all of my deepest and darkest thoughts because I was stupid enough to not just write them down but also to tell her about the existence of this book.

"Look, you don't have to worry, okay," Aurora says, putting her hand on mine as if she can read my mind. "I know that everything in that book is fiction. I mean, that's what writers do, right? Make things up?"

I wish, I want to say. But instead, I nod and say, "Of course."

PROBABLY SENSING MY UNEASINESS, Aurora answers the question that I asked her earlier.

"I've always wanted to own a boutique," she says. I stare at her trying to figure out what she's talking about.

"You asked me what I wanted to do as a girl and that's what I wanted to do. Curate a boutique. You know, pick out all the stuff for the store. Not just the clothes and the shoes and the accessories but all the other things as well. Journals. Cups. Paperclips."

"Your boutique would sell paper clips?" I ask. She furrows her brow and I realize how judgmental my question comes off.

"I really didn't mean it like that. I'm just imagining those packs of paper clips from Staples..." I explain. She laughs.

"No, nothing like *that*. I thought I would sell one big paper clip at a time, but it would have funny designs on it or funny or inspirational sayings. You know like *Boss Babe* or *It's Monday! Let's get stuff done!* Something like that."

"I really like that," I say after a moment. "You mean something like Francesca's?"

"Oh, that's one of my favorites!"

"Me, too!" I smile.

"Like Francesca's but also more my style."

"So, Aurora's?" I joke. She nods and laughs as well.

18

HARLEY

WHEN WE GET TO KNOW EACH OTHER...

M uch to what seems like both mine and Aurora's surprise, we end up talking well into the evening.

We order food and eat together, get to know each other without really putting in much effort.

We both come from very different places and yet when we talk to one another the conversation just flows.

If a lull does form, one of us is quick to fill it in before it becomes too big.

"I've never really had a girlfriend before," Aurora says. "Is this what it feels like?"

"What do you mean?"

"Well, you know, with your girlfriends, do you just sit around like this and bullshit all night long?"

"I've only really had one good friend who was a

girl and yes that's exactly what we did," I say slowly.

"What happened?"

I shrug.

I don't really want to go into it.

I'm cautious.

Just because I connected with her over the last few hours doesn't mean that she is someone I can actually trust.

But then I turn to her and see her big wide eyes waiting for me to answer and the words come to the tip of my tongue.

"I'm sorry, you don't have to tell me if you don't want to," she says quietly. "I mean, I know that we don't know each other very well."

I think about that for a moment.

She's right, of course.

But why the hell not? I have this tendency to take everything inside of me and keep it there.

And while this feels protective and safe, I'm not really sure that it is. What happened between Julie and me isn't a secret, so why treat it that way?

Unsure as to where to start, I start at the beginning. I tell her about Martin being my bodyguard and his relationship with my roommate.

And then I tell her about his death.

It feels good to talk about it again. Especially

with someone who isn't so intimately connected to the whole thing.

I know that Jackson probably wishes that I would open up to him, but it feels nice talking to Aurora.

She wasn't there.

She doesn't have her own experience of the situation.

She didn't know Julie and Martin, so it's easier for her to just be there and listen. And at this point, that's all I really want.

"I've always wanted to have a friendship like you and Julie did," Aurora says. "Just to have a girl to talk to about things. It's different than talking to a guy, or a therapist."

"I'm not really sure we have a friendship anymore."

"What do you mean?"

I shrug, looking down at the floor.

"Just give her some time, Harley. Someone just killed a man she loved. She probably just needs some time to grieve."

I nod, hanging my head. I hope she's right, but I am not really sure.

"You don't think so?" Aurora asks.

"I've never seen her have a connection like the one that she had with Martin. And now that he's gone?" I take a deep breath, trying to collect my thoughts. "He's dead because of me."

"No, he's not," Aurora says, shaking her head.

I roll my eyes. She takes a step closer to me, putting her hands on my shoulders.

"Look at me," she says. I refuse. She repeats herself again and again until I do.

Finally, I look up at her, reluctantly.

"Someone shot Martin and killed him. You didn't do that. You can't put that on yourself."

"But he wouldn't even be in that situation if it weren't for me."

"And he wouldn't be in that situation if he wasn't a bodyguard," Aurora corrects me.

On an intellectual level, I know that she's right. But on an intuitive level? Down in the pit of my stomach, I know that he's dead because of me.

"I really appreciate you saying all that, but I just need some time to come to grips with everything."

"Yes, I understand," she says, pulling herself away from me.

"Can I run something by you though?" I ask after a moment. She nods.

"It's something my mom mentioned. She thinks that it was probably Parker who was on the bike that night. And that it was he who shot Martin."

Aurora leans a little bit closer to me.

"Is that what you wanted to run by me?" she asks. "Do you not think it was Parker?"

I shrug.

"No, it probably was. Or, I don't know. I mean, he fit the general description but it all happened so fast, I don't really know."

Aurora eats a handful of blueberries out of the bowl she brought out of the refrigerator.

I take one, too.

It's so sour that it makes my whole face contort, but as soon as the taste dissipates I reach for another.

"There's something else she got me thinking about as well."

Aurora pops a blueberry in her mouth and waits.

"My mom suggested that it was Parker who leaked the story to the press about me being pregnant."

Aurora stops chewing for a moment, staring at me.

19

HARLEY

WHEN WE ARE INTERRUPTED...

"You knew that I was pregnant, right?" I ask.

She nods slowly. "Well, sort of. I mean, I saw that they said you were but I wasn't sure if it was true or not."

"It was. I lost the baby after the attack," I say the words slowly, trying to avoid taking myself to that dark place where all I have are flashbacks of what happened.

I don't want to talk about that, I want to talk about Parker.

"The only people who knew anything about this were Julie, Martin, and Jackson. And my doctor and the nurse staff at her office. But that was it."

"So...what are you getting at?"

"What I'm getting at is that Parker couldn't have known about the baby, right?"

"Journalists do have a way of finding things out, Harley. Okay, here are two possibilities. One possibility is that a journalist was just following you and Jackson around and wanted to get a good story and investigated this all on their own."

I nod. "That doesn't seem likely."

"Why not?"

"Because Jackson wasn't really in the news that much before. I mean, he was sort of but not enough for them to track him down and then get my medical records and do all of this investigating."

"I agree," Aurora says. "But there is someone who did have an incentive to track you."

"Parker."

"He's a stalker, in that real sense of the word. Just because no one knows where he is doesn't mean that he is any less interested in what you're doing. He may have been following you and then discovered that you went to the doctor. And then wondered why the hell would she go to see someone there? And that might have led him to finding out about your pregnancy."

"And that would've made him very angry," I say.

"It doesn't seem to take much," Aurora says.

"And then, what, he just went to the press about it?"

"He didn't have to go to the press, as you said. Not everyone would be interested in a story like that. But a few specific publications, like the ones owned by Minetta, would have been. And of course, the Post."

"But why? Why would he want them to know?"

"I'm not sure," Aurora says. "But I think he is getting a kick out of this. Being involved with you, and getting away with everything, is making him a much more powerful person than he ever was before."

There are a lot of what-ifs in this story, but something about it feels right. No one else would really have the incentive.

And the only other way any journalist would know about my pregnancy is if the medical staff just revealed it to them on purpose, without anyone coming to them with questions.

That seems like a very unlikely scenario.

"So, what do you know about Parker?" Aurora asks after a moment. Her question catches me by surprise.

"Actually, it's kind of funny to admit, but I don't really know anything."

She furrows her brow.

"I mean, I know how this whole thing started.

How he was in the beginning and then how things escalated in terms of him following me around, but when it comes to knowing anything specific about him, I really don't know much."

Aurora nods, running her finger around the outside of the blueberry bowl.

Saying this out loud really disturbs me.

How could this person be such a big part of my life and I know so little about him?

"It's so embarrassing to say, but I guess he scared me so much over all of this time that whenever he wasn't around, I didn't want to spend my time thinking about him. You know what I mean?"

She nods her head.

"You don't have to, I was just asking."

"No, you're right. You're absolutely right. I need to take control of this situation. That man has done so much to ruin my life and he'll keep going if I don't stop him."

"Harley...Aurora interrupts me. "That's not what I meant at all. I don't want you to do anything that would put you in harm's way.

"That's the thing though." I start to laugh. "Just being Harley Burke puts me in danger. He's out there. And no one knows where he is. But clearly, he is not anywhere far away, like the police suggested, because he rode up on a bike and fucking blew away my bodyguard!"

A pang of anger courses through my veins. I feel its ball of energy in the pit of my stomach and I feel nauseated.

"I just can't sit around and do nothing anymore. I mean, what more am I going to let that asshole take from me? He took my fucking child!"

Tears start to run down my face, and my whole body starts to shake. Aurora wraps her arms around me.

"What is going on here?" someone says, startling me.

"What did you say to her?" Jackson demands to know.

20

HARLEY

WHEN HE SHOWS UP...

Jackson takes me into his arms before I even have a moment to realize what is happening. He pushes Aurora away from me, turning me away from her as if she was the one who is responsible for my pain.

"I'm fine, everything is fine," I say, pushing away from him.

"Yes, I can see that," Jackson says. "What are you doing here?"

"I just stopped by-" She starts to say but he interrupts her.

"Why?"

"I needed someone to talk to."

"I am no longer that person."

Without saying another word, Jackson tugs on my shirt, trying to pull me out of the kitchen.

"What are you doing?"

"Let's go," he demands.

"No."

"Harley, let's go."

"No. What the hell are you doing?"

A man I don't recognize is standing before me. He looks like Jackson, but the anger that I see in his eyes doesn't belong to the man I knew before.

"What's going on?" I whisper. "Why are you so...?" My words trail off.

I am still feeling emotionally fragile and overwhelmed by the conversation with Aurora and I'm not entirely equipped to deal with this new Jackson.

"I am not anything, Harley," he snaps at me. "I just don't understand why I come home and find you and my ex-wife hanging out together."

"Well, she came over looking to talk to you. And you weren't here."

"So you just invited her in? As if that's...normal?"

"I don't know what's normal anymore, Jackson. My life isn't normal. She was here and we got to talking. And it was nice. It was nice to have someone to talk to."

"You can talk to me!" He raises his voice and it echoes in my mind.

"Yeah, right," I say under my breath, turning away from him.

"What? You can't?" he snaps again, grabbing my arm.

"Why don't you say that a little louder then?" I say, taking a step back.

"Listen, I am very sorry." Aurora tries to get in between us. "I really didn't mean to start anything."

"You didn't," I insist.

"Of course you did. You always do."

"Okay, let's just all calm down," I say after a moment. I feel this conversation going in circles without making much progress.

"Fine by me." Jackson walks over to the refrigerator and buries his head in there.

"I'm going to go," Aurora whispers to me.

"Wait, what? You're not going to stay the night?" I ask.

"It's not a good idea," she says calmly.

I walk her out to the foyer. I can't help but be a little bit disappointed.

"I had fun today," I say, handing her her coat.

"I did, too."

"You know, you can stay if you want. God knows this house is big enough."

She smiles.

"No, it's okay. It doesn't feel right. Jackson doesn't really want me here."

"That never stopped you before," I joke.

She laughs. I'm glad. When the words came out of my mouth, I immediately thought that it might be crossing the line.

"Where are you going to stay?" I ask.

"At the Ritz probably."

I nod.

"Hey, call me if you need anything, okay?" she says, taking my hand in hers. I give her a slight smile.

"Sure."

"You promise?" she asks.

"Yes, I promise."

After Aurora leaves, I go into kitchen to get my laptop and phone and then turn straight around to go upstairs.

"Are you even going to talk to me?" Jackson asks.

"Not when you're in such a bad mood."

"What did you expect?"

I stare at him, shaking my head.

"You don't get it, do you?" he asks. I shrug my shoulders and wait for him to explain.

"I come home and I find you hysterically crying. My ex-wife is here just standing there. I thought that she did something to hurt you."

I roll my eyes.

"No, that's what I really thought, Harley."

I take a deep breath, exhaling slowly.

"You don't believe me?"

"Don't be so dramatic, Jackson."

I turn away from him, but he follows me up the stairs.

"When she first showed up here, yes, I was a little confused. I didn't know why she just pops by like this. But she was really distressed. She had a big blow-up with Elliot, so we just talked about that."

"Fuckin' Elliot Woodward," Jackson says under his breath.

"Yes, that's the guy. So I tried to convince her that she can do a lot better than him. I'm not entirely sure if that worked, but we just got to talking about other things and it was nice."

"Like what?"

"Like Julie. I told her that Julie doesn't want to be my friend anymore and that she blames me for Martin's death."

"And Aurora made you feel better about that?"

I shrug. "It was just nice to tell someone, okay?"

"You could've told me."

"No, I couldn't. You're too...involved. Ever since that happened, there's this ocean between us. This space of everything that we should say to each other but we don't. All you do is work and all I do is anything but think about that night."

Jackson reaches for me, and this time I don't push him away. I'm standing a few steps above him, so when he pulls me closer, his chin is at my shoulders. I welcome him into my arms and we hold each other for a few minutes without saying a word.

"I'm so sorry about everything," Jackson says. "I'm sorry I didn't do more to...stop it."

"You couldn't have. You did everything right, Jackson. I don't blame you at all."

"I know you don't, but I blame myself."

"Well, you shouldn't."

21

JACKSON

WHEN I SHOW UP...

I am a stranger here.

Not in my house, but in her arms. I've never felt this way before. I never even felt this way when we first met.

But holding her now, pressing her body against mine, I feel like I don't belong with her. It's like I don't deserve her.

The shooting has pushed us so far apart that I worry that we will never get back to that other place.

She won't talk to me about what she's feeling and I can't tell her how I'm feeling either.

We both lost the baby but neither of us can really say a word about it to each other.

And then there's Martin.

I know that she blames herself for his death, and Julie blaming her for it as well isn't helping things.

But what can I do about it?

What can I do about it besides hold her close and pray that she believes the words that are coming out of my mouth?

Harley walks upstairs and I follow her.

Once we get to the master bedroom, I sit down on the bench at the far end of the bed and wait.

She puts down the laptop and her phone on the desk and sits down next to me.

"I don't know what to do," she admits.

"What do you mean?"

"I don't know what to do with myself. I feel so... bad...all the time."

I'm tempted to tell her not to feel this way, but I catch myself from saying this at the very last minute.

What hubris, right?

Who the hell am I to tell anyone how they should or shouldn't feel? No, all I can do at this moment is just listen and be there for her.

"I am just so sorry that it happened," I whisper.

"Me, too," she agrees. "And I'm so angry."

"Me, too."

We sit for a moment, leaning on each other,

and listening to each other's breath. We lost something we never knew we even wanted and it will take a long time to get over it, if ever.

"What can we do now?" she asks.

"I don't know. Just take it one moment at a time. Then one hour at a time. Then one day at a time?"

She shrugs. "That's not good enough."

"I don't know another way."

I hold her in my arms for a while until it feels right to pull away.

"Are you really mad about me being friends with Aurora?"

This takes me by surprise. It's hard to answer that. The thing is that I don't even really want to be friends with her, but that's really my own problem.

"I'm not really sure that she would be the best friend you could have," I finally say. She narrows her eyes, scrutinizing me.

"Why is that?"

"Aurora is a difficult person to be around. She is kind of a taker. She always has these problems that she comes and dumps into my lap."

"If you don't like that, why did you put up with it for so long?" Harley asks.

I don't really know how to answer this question.

We have a history together.

We lost a child.

We have known each other for a very long time and for many years when I closed myself off from the world, it was nice to know that there was someone out there who cared about me.

Harley waits, but I don't tell her any of these things. Instead, I just shrug and wall myself off from her.

"Why do you even want to be friends with her?"

"I'm not sure if I do," she says. "But it was nice talking to her today."

"I just don't want you to get hurt," I say.

But the truth is that that's only partly true.

I'm also afraid. Just the thought of my ex-wife hanging out with the woman I want to make my future wife makes me sick to my stomach.

There is nothing that I'm hiding from either one of them, and yet, imagining them spending time together like they did today on a more consistent basis - just throws my whole world into turmoil.

"There's something you need to know," I say, taking a deep breath. "She tried to kiss me again."

"When?"

"When you were gone."

Harley wants to know the details and I tell her every last one. I don't hold anything back. She listens patiently and pulls her hand away from mine.

"I stopped it right away. I didn't even linger for a moment."

"Why did she do that?"

"Because she needs someone to care about her. No matter how much someone loves her, it's never enough. And the men she is choosing to be with don't even give her a little bit of what she needs."

Harley nods and walks around the room, wrapping her hands around her arms.

"Do you miss her?" she asks after a moment.

"No. Absolutely not."

She nods in that way that isn't entirely convincing.

I walk over to her and pull her toward me. At first, she resists, but then she lets me in.

"I love you, Harley. I love you so much and that's why I told you. Because I didn't want there to be any secrets between us."

She nods. I don't think she gets it. I lift up her chin toward mine, focusing my gaze on hers. For a moment, I lose myself in the beauty of her irises.

"I love you, too," she whispers, pressing her lips onto mine.

As soon as our mouths collide, a powerful sensation courses through my entire body all at once.

I want her.

I crave her.

I'm going to scream if I don't have her right this minute. I walk backward toward the bed and pull her on top of me.

She gives off a little moan and I quickly move her underneath me.

22

JACKSON

WHEN WE GET CLOSE…

Our mouths weld to each other's and separate only briefly when we gasp for breath. My body feels strong and powerful against hers, while hers is small and soft in that good way.

The clothes that I'm wearing suddenly become an impediment and I can't wait to get them off me.

Leaning to one side doesn't do much good, so I jump up onto my knees, straddling her and pull off my shirt.

She runs her fingers down my abs, which I flex for her benefit. She smiles and licks her lips.

I stand up and pull her up to a sitting position. But when I tug at her shirt, she cowers away from me.

"What's wrong?" I ask, putting my lips onto hers again.

"Nothing," she mumbles.

I try to pull off her shirt again, but again she blocks me. I pull away slightly to take a look at her face. Her eyes refuse to meet mine.

"I'm sorry," she says, pushing me out of the way and getting off the bed.

I give her some space.

After waiting a few minutes, I walk over to her slowly. She is standing in front of the floor-to-ceiling window, staring at the bright lights of Manhattan. This is a quiet residential street, but there's nothing really peaceful about it.

"It's too soon," Harley says quietly.

I know what she means.

It's too soon to do that after what happened at the hospital.

It's too soon be intimate after losing so much. I was expecting that. The doctor told me that it can take six weeks or more for her to feel normal again.

But when the moment happened, all of that information flew out of my mind and I just lost myself in her body.

I nod, wrapping my arms around her. I am thankful that she doesn't push me away.

We stand staring at the trees below us and watch as three teenage girls laugh and skip across the street.

I can't hear what they're saying, but I sense their carefree spirit and I hope that one day I will feel as free as they do in this moment.

"Thanks for telling me about Aurora trying to kiss you," Harley finally says. "I believe you."

"Thank you for trusting me," I say, giving her a peck on the cheek.

―――――

WE STAND LEANING against each other for a while.

"I've been thinking about something," she says after a moment.

"What?" I ask, enjoying the feel of her head against my shoulder.

"I don't know anything about Parker."

I shrug, not really understanding why this matters one way or another.

"He knows so much about me, but I don't know anything about him."

"Why do you even want to?"

"I need to find him."

Her words come out softly, but with determination. I pull away from her, not certain if I can trust my ears. Did I really just hear that? Did she really just say that?

I wait for her to explain, but she doesn't. She

just stares into space, lost somewhere in the lights below.

"What are you talking about?" I finally ask. Harley looks up at me. The expression on my face, contorted and tense, takes her by surprise.

"What?" she asks as if she hadn't just dropped a bomb on me.

"What do you mean you need to find Parker?"

"When Aurora and I were talking, she asked me about Parker. Who he is, where he's from. Just basic facts. And the thing is that I didn't know the answers."

"So what? Who cares?"

"How could I know so little about this person who knows everything about me? Who stalked me? Who kidnapped me?"

"What does it matter?" I ask, taking a step away from her, unsure how to react.

"Well, he knows everything about me. He watches. And my way of dealing with him this whole time was to just put him out of my mind. And that's not right."

Everything that she is saying is something that I've thought about before. We do know very little about him and that's not the best way to deal with the enemy. Especially now that he has gone on the offensive again.

But I can't allow her to put herself in danger in order to find him. He has hurt her enough already.

"I don't think it's a very good idea for you to try to find out all of these things," I say as calmly as possible. But her eyes still flare up at me.

"I don't really care," she snaps.

"It's not safe, Harley."

"It's not safe doing what I'm doing now."

"So...what is your plan?"

"I'm going to try to research him. He's an enemy and the way to fight him is to understand him the best that I can."

I clench my jaw, shaking my head.

"Don't you understand? I don't know anything about him besides that he used to read my blog. I mean, don't you find that a bit strange?"

I shrug.

"I used to think that he was going to stop. One of these days he will find another hobby and just stop, but I don't think that's going to happen anymore."

I don't want to say it out loud, but I agree with her. I know she's right. Parker Huntington is obsessive and he won't let up until he gets what he wants. What he wants is Harley.

"It's not that I don't agree with you," I say slowly. "It's just that I don't want you to get hurt."

She rolls her eyes at first, but then adds, "I know."

"Do you understand?" I ask, taking a step closer to her and putting my hands on her shoulders. "I love you. I nearly lost you twice. I can't let you do this."

"You can't let me? Who the hell do you think you are?" Harley says, pulling away from me.

23

JACKSON

WHEN WE FIGHT...

I immediately regret my choice of words, but not the meaning. I will do everything in my power to protect her.

Even though, at this point, it doesn't feel like there is much that I can do.

"You know what I mean," I say.

"No, I don't. I really don't, Jackson. I mean, he kidnapped me, almost killing me. He killed Martin. He made me lose our child. What more do you need him to do?"

Her words make my blood curl. Does she really think that I don't care? Does she really think that I would just let him do all of these things without repercussion?

"I don't know where he is, Harley. I want nothing more than to wrap my hands around his throat and hold on tightly until I vanquish every bit of life in him."

"So do I," she says, narrowing her eyes.

We stand staring at each other, knowing one another's grief. Within a moment, my grief turns to anger, roiling around in the pit of my stomach. I look down at my hands and I realize that they are balled up into fists.

"I don't want you getting involved with this," I say after a moment.

"I don't know what kind of bubble you are living in, but I am already involved. This is all because of me. Martin is dead because of me."

"No, he's dead because he was a bodyguard."

"Yeah, hired to protect me."

"So, if anything, he is dead because of me," I say. "I was the one who hired him."

She glares at me. I stare back at her.

"And what about our baby?" she asks. "He or she is dead because of me."

Tears start to roll down her face. I pull her close to me. She pushes away at first, but then her body goes limp, falling into my arms.

I don't know where to go from here. I know that we are both angry, but I am also scared. I am petrified of what will happen if I can't protect her. And I know that I can't.

"I am just really afraid of losing you," I whisper over and over again.

———————————

THE FOLLOWING MORNING, things between Harley and me are not much improved. We are cordial and polite but there's a tension that I never felt before.

I know that we should talk about what happened more and what she plans on doing, if anything, but I have an important meeting this morning and I don't have time to start an in-depth conversation.

Nor do I have the energy.

Besides Parker Huntington, there's another pressing issue on my mind. Andrew Lindell.

He is the asshole who forced me to sell Minetta.

I thought that selling my shares would be the end of our involvement but he is pressing me into service.

I have no interest in running a company as a CEO for hire, but if I don't then he will fire every employee there just to spite me.

I used to love my job.

I used to look forward to getting up each day and trying to figure out how to make the company bigger and into what content areas we should expand.

But now that I am no longer a part of it, now that I am forced to work there, I dread it.

Every email that I get from Avery Phillips feels like an anchor that's pulling me further and further down to the bottom of the ocean.

I am doing my best to try to make things right there, to make the best decisions for Minetta, but it all just seems to pull me closer and closer to drowning. Minetta isn't doing well and Lindell knows it.

Now, I have to meet with him and explain.

I arrive at the meeting at the most expensive steakhouse in Manhattan right on time, and not a moment early.

I expect Andrew to make me wait, in some sort of power move, but am surprised to see that he is already here.

The look on his face is so pleasant that he actually appears to be happy to see me.

After a firm handshake and a few pleasantries, I take my seat right across from him and open the wine menu.

He recommends a red that I've never tried before and the sommelier brings it out for me to taste.

"I'll take a glass of that, thank you," I say, turning my attention to the menu.

"The filet mignon is delicious here," he says.

"I don't know if you know, but I don't eat meat," I say. This takes him by surprise and that surprises me.

"Oh, I had no idea."

I don't know if he's lying, but I get the sense that he isn't. When he invited me here, I thought that he just didn't care.

"Would you like to go somewhere else?" he asks. From what I know about him, he isn't the most accommodating person in the world. So, I'm not quite sure where this is all coming from. I scan the menu quickly.

"No, it's fine," I say. "I'll get the salmon. I eat fish, eggs, and vegetables, of course. Just not meat."

24

JACKSON

AT LUNCH...

"Is there any particular reason you don't eat meat?" Andrew asks.

"Welfare of animals," I say without missing a beat. "I'm planning on cutting out dairy as well."

I expect him to ask me more about it, but he doesn't. Instead, he gives me his condolences for what happened to Martin and Harley.

"Thank you. I appreciate you saying that."

"So, how is Harley doing now?"

"As well as can be expected."

I know that we are not here to talk about Harley and I want to get to the point as quickly as possible, but I also don't want to be unnecessarily rude. I do technically work for him and it's in my best interest to keep things pleasant.

He asks me more questions about the attack

and I answer them as succinctly as I can without providing too much of an explanation. I keep trying to pivot the conversation to something else but he keeps bringing it back to this.

Finally, when our food arrives, I say, "I appreciate you asking about Harley and everything that we have gone through, but I am certain that's not why you invited me here."

"Well, then you would be wrong," Andrew says, leaning back in his chair. I narrow my eyes. What does he mean by this?

"The thing is that Minetta isn't doing well, as you know."

I shrug, nodding. "I am doing my best to turn things around."

"Yes, actually, I am aware of that. Thank you."

He cuts into his steak and takes a bite. I wait for him to continue.

"We've been in contact with a public relations firm that will allow us to raise the profile of the company in general. Build more sympathy and public awareness of what it is that we do here."

"Plenty of people listen to our podcasts and read our articles," I say.

"Yes, plenty of people do, but most don't. There was a recent poll about that. Outside of those who are highly educated and politically inclined individuals, few are even aware of what a podcast is."

I know the article that he is citing and I know that this is a big problem.

The reason why most podcasts are about politics is that that's who the listeners are.

And that's precisely why most people who aren't interested in politics don't have any podcasts to listen to that would be of interest.

"Anyway, it was the PR people's idea that we use what happened to you as a way to raise Minetta's profile in the media."

I furrow my brows.

"So, that's why all of those articles came out about the shooting right afterward?"

He nods.

"I am sorry about that, but I hope that the media spotlight will do some good as well. From what I hear, Parker Huntington, Harley's kidnapper, is still at large. Perhaps all of this media coverage can help capture him."

I'll give Andrew Lindell one thing. He certainly does his homework.

"Why do I get the feeling that you are about to ask me a favor?" I ask, taking a bite of my salad.

"Well, it's not so much a favor as a request," Andrew says, smiling out of the corner of his mouth.

I sit back and wait.

"Now that we have established interest in you as the CEO of Minetta and this horrible thing that has happened to your girlfriend and unborn child, we need to give the public something to root for."

I drop my fork to the floor.

When it hits the tile, it makes a loud dinging sound, startling him for a moment. Did he just say what I think he said? I stare at him waiting for him to continue but he doesn't.

"What do you mean 'you established interest in Minetta?' Did you tell them about Harley being pregnant?"

"Well, not me personally," he says with a satisfied expression on his face.

I shake my head.

"What are you telling me exactly?" I ask.

He tilts his head and smiles. "Jackson, I think you know."

"How did they even know about her pregnancy?"

"You work for us and we have very good people in charge of our investigations."

"But why were you even investigating us?"

"Jackson, it is our job to know what is going on in our employees' lives. Especially those as powerful and high up as you are."

"So...you followed her?"

"Yes, we followed her," he says as if he hadn't done anything wrong. "Of course. And when the investigator reported that she was going to an OB-GYN then we did a further investigation and discovered that she was indeed pregnant with your child."

I clench my fists in anger. Who does this guy think he is? But when my eyes meet his, I realize that he is not cowering at this news at all. He doesn't even think that he did anything wrong.

"You can't do that," I say. "You can't just invade my girlfriend's privacy like this."

"Well, maybe not, but I did," he says smugly. I want to punch him in his arrogant face, and I grab the table to stop myself from actually doing it.

25

JACKSON

LATER AT LUNCH...

Harley thinks that it was Parker who followed her to the doctor's office and then leaked her pregnancy to the press, but it was actually Lindell this whole time.

Why is he so paranoid?

Why is he involved in my personal life?

I am angry and I am tempted to storm off but doing that isn't going to get me the answers I need.

Then something else occurs to me. Is he tapping my phone? Does he have listening devices or even cameras in my house? I have no idea.

"I know that you probably think that this is a big invasion of privacy but it's all for the general good," Andrew insists.

"And who is benefiting from knowing that my unborn child is gone?"

"Are you seriously asking me this?" He looks at me as if I have lost my mind. "Minetta, of course."

I shake my head.

"Everyone feels bad for you now. It helps a lot that you two make quite a beautiful couple."

I clench my jaw.

"Anyway, everyone is really sad for you now, as you can imagine, and many are now looking into what the hell is Minetta anyway? Our page views are up twenty percent. The podcast subscription rates are up almost thirty."

"This is not how you do business," I say.

"This is precisely how you do business," he snaps. "The CEO is the public face of the company. Especially if he is attractive and has a story of his own to tell. This is going to make a lot more people interested in our public offering and make the offer a lot more lucrative."

I stare at him, not saying a word.

"Look, I know that you're not a fan of any of this. I know that you hate your job right now."

"If you know that, then why don't you let me go?"

"I was thinking about that. Of course, I don't want you to work where you don't want to. But I just can't. You are too important. Without you, there's no Minetta."

"So, I will have to work here indefinitely?" I ask.

"I wouldn't say that."

I feel my body perk up.

"Listen, I want to let you go, I do. I don't enjoy forcing anyone to do anything against their will, but I also need to think about my goals. Especially for Minetta."

I don't say anything, instead I wait for him to explain where I come in.

"I need the company to go public so that I can cash out of it and let the investors take over. But as you know it's not doing too well. So, we first need to raise its profile and its subscribers and unique page clicks."

"I know all of this already," I point out. I have no idea why he's repeating himself as if I am not clued in.

"Don't be rude," he snaps at me. I don't apologize. "You want me to get to the point?"

"Yes, please," I say.

"Fine. The point is that I need you to ask Harley to marry you."

This takes me by complete surprise. I sit back in my seat and stare at him.

"C'mon, don't pretend you didn't want to."

"I have no idea what you're talking about," I insist.

"My investigators have informed me that you

actually got her a ring already. Three carats, was it? That's nice! You were going to propose."

The one thing that I find particularly shocking is how nonchalant he is being with the fact that he has had his CEO under surveillance this whole time. It's as if it's a normal thing to do.

"What does my engagement have to do with anything?"

"Oh, I thought you didn't want me to explain?" he mocks me. "I thought that you knew everything already."

"Please explain," I say through my teeth.

"You and Harley have both been through so much recently. The public knows that and they are sympathetic. But now we have to give them something to root for. A beautiful engagement sounds like the perfect way to go."

I shake my head.

"Listen, if you want, I can put you with an event planner who will arrange everything. Or you can do it yourself. But what we mostly care about is to be there to capture the moment with our photographers and videographers. Minetta blogs and online magazines will be the first ones to report on the story and after that it will be everywhere."

"But what's the point?" I ask.

"This is a feel-good story that will go a long way

to raising Minetta's profile through you, its charismatic CEO. Maybe we can even arrange for some interviews on the morning talk shows and evening cable news shows."

I shake my head.

"C'mon, Jackson." Andrew puts his hand on my arm as if we are close friends. I recoil from his touch. "You were going to ask her to marry you anyway. This way, we'll just be there to capture the moment and share the good news with the world."

26

HARLEY

WHEN I START TO TAKE THE INITIATIVE...

Jackson doesn't want me to go on the offensive but it's not really up to him.

If he doesn't want to help me, that's one thing.

I don't need his help.

I can do all of this on my own.

We leave things off on a standstill.

Neither of us are happy but neither of us are willing to budge in one direction or another. While he goes to lunch with Andrew Lindell, I sit down at my work desk and instead of writing, I start researching.

It's hard to know where to start since I don't have much experience with this. But I have watched plenty of episodes of Catfish so I start with social media. He must have some sort of social media presence, right?

I search for his name.

There are more than twenty different Parker Huntingtons on Facebook.

I search for his name in connection to my kidnapping on Google and find out from the online magazine stories that he is from Missoula, Montana.

Montana, really?

That can't be a coincidence, right? What is it that the cops say, there are no coincidences?

How could I not have known this before? He is from my hometown and I never connected the dots until right now?

I hate myself for procrastinating on this for so long.

I know exactly why I did it, but it still feels like shit. It's hard to know what every little piece of information would add up to and, on the surface, it doesn't feel like it's a big deal that he's from Missoula.

But the more I think about it, the angrier I get.

Mainly, at myself. If I had just looked into this before.

If I had just not averted my eyes from the truth, who knows what I could've prevented.

I feel sick to my stomach thinking that I could've saved our baby's life and didn't.

I'm tempted to distract myself and do something else instead. But I force myself to keep going. You have to find out more. You have to work until you hit a dead end and then work even harder, I say to myself.

I search for Parker's name on Facebook and find one from Missoula. It's all set to private so I make a fake account with a fake name and find a picture of a pretty girl with long blonde hair online.

This girl will be my stand-in.

As soon as I make a few posts and friend a few people, I friend Parker and wait.

In the meantime, I try to look him up on other social media. I look up on Google whether I can find his Instagram from his Facebook profile and it says that I can, but only if we are friends.

I wonder if he's on Twitter but read that it's even harder to look that up if I just know his Facebook. While I wait, I turn my attention to Sam.

I friend him, too, and he accepts my request almost simultaneously. My heart skips a beat as I start to look at his profile.

He doesn't update much but he does have his Instagram listed and I hope there are more pictures on there. His pictures are organized into albums and as I scroll through them, I spot one called Montana.

I inhale deeply before clicking on it.

In the middle of all the pictures of pines reaching toward the bright blue sky and lakes with water like glass, I see one of him and Parker, standing on a rock, with their arms wrapped around each other's shoulders. It's from a number of years ago.

They both look rather young, maybe high school age? Maybe just out of their teens.

"So, they have known each other all of this time," I whisper to myself in disbelief.

"How did you know each other?" I look through the other pictures, but there's nothing else there that would give me a clue as to the answer.

I check back with my profile and see that Parker has actually friended me. Score! I search through his albums, eventually finding a similar picture of the two of them. However, his has a caption.

MY FRIEND SAM *visiting from New York!*

I RETURN to the Google results of Sam, and after all of the various arrests and court documents that I have to pay to access, I find something unexpected. It's a newspaper article from his high school.

Luckily, they scanned all of their articles and made them available online.

Reading through the article, I learn that Sam won an essay contest for the National Park Service and won a six-week internship that was based out of Missoula. I am not sure if Parker participated in the same internship or not, but that's probably how they met.

I continue my search for close to two hours, seeking every article that I find at all relevant to their lives.

I read each one and then carefully write down notes on relevant pieces of information.

Well, relevant isn't exactly the right word. I have no idea what would be relevant to where they are now.

But I do know that I need to know more. I need to know who they really are.

When I click back to the front of Parker's account, I notice something that I hadn't noticed before. It's right there and yet, I somehow overlooked it. Under education, he lists Aspen Valley High School.

That's where I went. Is this for real?

According to this, he graduated two years behind me.

But this can't be real, right?

I went to a large suburban school with a graduating class of close to four hundred students. I didn't even know many in my own class, let alone those two years behind me. But he must've known me, right?

Hey there.

A message pops up at the bottom of my computer screen. It's from Parker. My heart skips a beat. He is actually messaging me.

Hey, I message him back.

27

HARLEY

WHEN WE TALK...

My fingers turn to ice as I wait for him to reply, eager to get the conversation started.

I never message strangers on here, but you're so pretty...I couldn't help myself.

Thanks, I never message strangers either, I write.

Yeah, right. :-) You did friend a stranger.

I send a shrug emoji.

As we can continue to banter back and forth, I quickly make Instagram and Twitter accounts.

I populate the Instagram with some pictures of the girl I used for my Facebook and also a bunch of pictures of appetizing looking salads and wildlife shots.

I write short captions and follow over a

hundred people who use pretty generic tags, hoping that they will follow me back.

I probably need at least twenty followers to make the account look somewhat legitimate.

So where are you from, Dani?

I freeze. What do I say? I want to make up a completely different location, but I'm pretty sure that my location is geotagged with Instagram. Plus, the best lies are those that are closest to the truth.

Tristate area, I write.

Which one?

New York, New Jersey?

Yep.

Which one?

Sorry, I can't be more specific right now. I don't even know you.

I get it, he writes.

When I ask him where he is right now, he is just as opaque. His answer is just two words: New England.

That's even less specific than what I said.

Well, I don't really know you.

I don't push it. I keep the conversation friendly.

We talk about movies and music and the weather. It's nothing in particular, but it's important. We are building a rapport and maybe that can lead to something else.

While we talk, I try to look him up on Twitter.

But I don't know his handle and it's not under his Facebook name.

So, I Google how to find Facebook friends on Twitter and one of the first search results takes me to the step by step instructions.

It's a bit more of a complicated process. First, I have to make a Yahoo Mail account. I make it to match my fake Facebook name and then log in and click on Contact at the top left.

Then I import contacts and get the option to import contacts from Facebook and other platforms.

Then, I log into Twitter, click on 'Discover' and then Find Friends at the top left. I click on the 'Search Contacts' button and a few seconds later, his name appears.

The website says this only works if his privacy is set up in a particular way, and luckily it is. I start scrolling through his Twitter.

Unlike the friendly images that populate his Facebook, his Twitter account is another beast altogether.

There are retweets from various white nationalist pages as well as many misogynist, xenophobic, and homophobic tweets.

He calls many women politicians the c-word and many African American actors the n-word. His

page is populated with so many f-word
homophobic slurs that it makes my skin crawl.

Why didn't I take a few minutes to look
him up?

How did I not know this before?

As I read through all of his garbage, I discover
that he lost his job a few years ago at a big box
store for cursing at his boss, whom he referred to
by both the c-word and the n-word, and then
posted tweets about stockpiling guns and
ammunition.

So, what do you do for a living? Parker messages.

I think about it for a moment and then decide
to give us something to connect over.

Work at Bed Bath & Beyond, I write.

Fucking hate those stores, no offense.

Why?

Used to work at Walmart.

What happened?

*My boss was a total bitch, to say the least. I was
late only a few times and she wouldn't let me slide at
all. Just only got her job because of affirmative action
anyway.*

He doesn't know me so I get the feeling that
he's more polite than usual. But I egg him on
saying that my boss is the same way.

Once I give him permission and he sees that
I'm on his side, he lets all of his feelings out.

He calls his boss every slur he can think of, but I don't even blink. My goal is to make him my friend. I have to make him comfortable with me. I want him to be real. Maybe then I can connect with him.

You know I'm really surprised, most girls would be offended by what I just said, he points out.

I'm not like most girls.

I'm getting that sense.

When I send him a smiling face emoji, he asks, *Want to video chat?*

Shit. This is what I've been afraid of. I can't video chat because he knows what I look like. But I have to finesse this situation.

I could lie and tell him that my camera doesn't work or something lame like that but I don't want to put him on alert. Maybe being vulnerable is the way to go for now. That way I can buy myself some time.

No, I don't feel comfortable yet.

I totally understand. Sorry, didn't mean to make you feel that way.

I'm surprised by his statement. He is much more receptive than I thought he would be.

When he takes the conversation back to my work, I decide that the best way to part is to leave him wanting more. I have to be the first to say good-bye.

Speaking of work, I actually have to get back now. I'll talk to you later.

Oh...okay. Really, I didn't mean to offend you, he writes.

I feel the desperation in his voice and it makes me smile.

I have the upper hand.

No worries. It was nice talking with you.

Yeah, same here.

I consider writing something else, but instead I close the window. That's enough for now.

The wave of nausea comes over me all of a sudden like a tornado. I barely make it to the toilet to throw up.

28

JACKSON

WHEN HE MAKES ANOTHER OFFER...

It has been a few weeks since Andrew Lindell asked me to propose to Harley. I know that doing this will go a long way to getting him off my back, but I don't want to.

At first, he calls me a few times, reminding me of the request in a polite tone. But after a while, his requests turn more into demands. I avoid a few of his calls while I try to figure out what to do.

On one hand, he is right.

I already have the ring and I do want to propose to Harley. I've been waiting for the right moment and perhaps doing it in a public way isn't the worst idea.

On the other hand, however, I don't want her to think that the only reason I proposed was to raise Minetta's profile.

I could try to keep it a secret, but not only would that make me feel like a total asshole, it would also be something that would mar our engagement and marriage.

There have been enough lies and secrets in our relationship, and I don't want to lie to her ever again.

"I'm glad you finally answered me," Andrew Lindell says on the other end of the phone.

"Listen, I know what you want, but I can't do it," I say. I only picked up the phone because I didn't recognize the number and I'm surprised to hear his voice.

"I know that I probably haven't given you enough of the *right* kind of incentive," he says smugly. "I can see that the stick doesn't work on you, so why don't we try a carrot then?"

"What are you talking about?" I ask, pacing around the room.

"Well, what if I were to tell you where you could find Parker Huntington?"

I stop mid-step, nearly tripping over my foot.

"I thought that would get your attention," he says. I wait for him to continue. "Hello? Are you there?" he asks after a moment.

"Yes, I'm here. You know where Parker is?"

"Yes, we do."

"And you're not telling the police or the FBI?"

"Nope."

"Why?"

"Because, we don't really have a good reason to follow him and we don't need them breathing down our neck."

"Why were you following him in the first place?"

"I like to collect surveillance on people who are connected to people who work for me, just in case I ever need to use it."

He may be lying, but he may also be telling the truth.

"How much is that information worth to you, Jackson?"

A lot, I say to myself.

"Yeah, I thought so.".," Andrew laughs on the other end of the phone, reading my mind.

"So, what are you telling me exactly?" I ask.

"You propose to Harley in a lavish, ultra-romantic way and allow our cameras to record the whole thing for the tabloids and in exchange I will tell you the exact location where you can find Parker Huntington."

"And why would I want to know that?"

"Why wouldn't you? He's the man responsible for kidnapping your girlfriend and almost killing her, killing your friend and your unborn child. No one knows where he is. Are you really telling me that you don't want to get your hands on that asshole and put a bullet in his head?"

"I am not a violent man," I say, even though he's right. That's precisely what I want to do with him. Or maybe even worse.

"No one is until circumstances require them to be."

I take a deep breath processing exactly what he is telling me.

"No one will know about this. No one will know that this conversation even took place."

"Except that we are on the phone together," I point out.

"I'm on a burner phone. That's why you didn't recognize my number and picked up." He laughs.

I still don't reply.

"Why don't I paint you a little picture?" Andrew continues. "You have this beautiful proposal where the love of your life agrees to marry you. And to celebrate, you will get to the precise place where Parker Huntington is sleeping safely in his bed, shoot him in the head with an untraceable gun, and vanish into the night. You and I both know that the world would be a much better place without him in it, especially Harley's."

Every impulse in my body yearns for this. I can see myself doing it exactly as he has described and my mouth practically salivates at the idea. I am not a criminal and I'm not one to take the law into my own hands, but the police and the FBI have betrayed us. They promised to find him and they haven't. They promised to keep Harley safe and they haven't.

"You and I both know that Harley will never be safe while he is out there, walking around free," he says, reading my mind.

"Maybe not, but that doesn't mean that I can take this matter into my own hands," I say. I say this because it's the right thing to say, in case anyone is listening. I don't know if he can tell that, but it doesn't matter.

"What you do then is up to you. You can call the police and they can arrest him for you, and probably let him go with time served," Andrew mocks me.

I don't say anything in response.

"Okay, how about this. Think about it and let me know. But I hope that you know that there's only one answer that I'll accept."

Andrew hangs up, leaving me in a state of limbo. I stare at the phone until it goes black.

My mind runs in circles until I get dizzy. I sit down and try to collect my thoughts. What Andrew just offered me is a gift bigger than I ever thought I would ever get. I don't even know if he knows what it is that he is offering me.

Parker Huntington's life is now in my hands. I am the only person now who can avenge what he did to Martin and my unborn child.

It's also up to me to make sure that he never hurts Harley again.

29

JACKSON

WHEN I DECIDE...

I know that his obsession with her will never stop until his lifeless body is deep underground, but I also know that I need to be careful.

I don't know if anyone is tapping my phone.

It is not likely but I will not be one of those fools whose recorded conversations are blasted all over the courtroom at their trial. No, Parker is the one who should be on trial.

He is the one who is responsible for all of this and it's him who will pay.

But what about waiting for the police to get him? What about allowing time for the prosecutor's office to make their case?

It's tempting, of course.

But then again, how many chances should we give them?

I've waited for them to make the case against Sam and all they did was let him go. I don't know how much they have on Parker, if anything, and if they don't have any evidence of him being the man on the bike then he will not get a life sentence for executing Martin.

Whatever time he would serve for kidnapping Harley wouldn't be enough.

I wait until the evening to call him back with my decision.

"How do I know that you will let me know where he is located after I ask her to marry me?" I ask when he answers the phone.

"I'll have our investigator escort you to him."

A smile comes over my face. "Perfect."

ANDREW'S EVENT planner has all sorts of suggestions for how to plan the perfect proposal and I listen to her carefully as she goes into all the details.

Apparently, nowadays, proposals can be as lavish as rehearsal dinners with parties being organized and thrown afterward.

I don't want anything like that, but I have no idea if Harley does.

On the surface, she seems like an easy going girl with not too many requests. But when it comes to a wedding proposal, who the hell knows?

Maybe she does want something fancy and beautiful.

Maybe she does want me to go the extra mile to make her feel special.

The one thing that I am pretty certain of is that she does not want this to be a staged situation in exchange for information on Parker Huntington.

But she doesn't have to know.

That's something that I am doing for her, even if she hasn't asked me to.

Parker Huntington has been a threat to her for way too long. He has tried to hurt her numerous times and has succeeded on occasion. How many more chances am I willing to take?

The answer is that I'm not willing to take any more chances.

So, even though I know that this is probably the last thing that she wants, I'm going to go through with it. I want her to be my wife, and God-willing, I will take this whole thing to my grave after seventy years of a happy marriage.

TWO MORE WEEKS pass as we plan the event. By we, I mean, mainly the event planner.

I am too busy with work to pay much attention but she does tell me when and where to show up.

I write it down in my calendar along with a note reminding me to bring the engagement ring.

Harley never goes into my work laptop so I'm certain that this info is safe here.

Besides, Harley has been quite busy at work as well. She is working hard on finishing the latest novel, which readers will be snapping up as soon as it goes live.

She has become quite an expert at Facebook advertising, and is even increasing the spend.

It's something that I had encouraged her to do ever since she started, but it's something that she's only now doing since she has gained more confidence in the process.

She keeps promising to pay me back every last cent that she spends and keeps a pretty accurate spreadsheet of all of her costs.

At first, I thought that this was just an empty promise, but given how many people are buying her books, it's probably going to happen.

I keep saying to myself that as soon as we marry, my money will become her money, but I doubt that I will be able to convince her of that, even if she were to say yes.

That's the thing, though. No matter how lavish the proposal and how beautiful the setting, Harley still has to say yes. And I'm not sure if she will.

I love her and she says she loves me, too.

But ever since we got back from the hospital, things haven't been the same.

We both lost something that night, something irreplaceable and I'm not sure if we have recovered. No, that's a lie. Nothing has been the same since then.

30

JACKSON

LATER...

Weeks pass in oblivion.
We spend time together but nothing is really the same.

She cries a lot and I cry as well, but somewhere apart from her. I am afraid to show her that I am hurting, too.

Why?

It's hard to explain.

Probably because I don't want to make this real to myself. I hide my pain and it makes it feel less acute.

But then one day, I wake up and I feel lighter. It's hard to say that I feel lighter, it's more that the weight that has been pressing down on me isn't as heavy all of a sudden.

That evening we decide to order takeout and watch something together in the living room.

I've spent so much time buried in work that it's nice to sit and do nothing.

Dressed in sweatpants and a loose-fitting V-neck sweater, Harley comes downstairs looking like an angel.

Her hair cascades down around her shoulders and it moves in slow waves with each step.

When she sits down next to me, she takes my hand into hers and gives me a little smile.

"I missed you," I whisper and she nods.

Her face glows in the evening light.

Her eyes are wide and gorgeous, but the sorrow that has settled into them is gone for now.

I am sure that it is still there, just below the surface.

"I missed you, too," she says.

"I really want to go back to the way things were, you know?" I ask.

When the words come out of my mouth, they sound callous and cold. But I look at her and realize that she knows exactly what I mean.

"I do, too," she says. "It happened and, of course, I want to take every part of it back, but I also don't want to lose you."

"You don't?"

"No, I love you. I don't want to lose the one

person who means everything in the world to me," she says quietly. "That man has done enough to ruin my life and I'm not going to let him ruin this."

She doesn't say his name and I appreciate that.

"I won't let him," I say quietly. "I love you, Harley."

"I love you, too," she whispers, putting her arm around my neck and kissing me just below my ear lobe.

I press my lips onto hers. Her mouth opens wide, inviting me in. I bury my hands in her hair, tugging lightly until she moans from pleasure.

"I missed you," she whispers. "I missed you so much."

"I did, too," I mumble as my mouth makes its way down her neck. She throws her head back and I move loose strands of hair off her collarbone.

My right hand makes its way under her shirt and up toward her breasts. She's not wearing a bra and her breasts welcome my touch. I run my fingers over her nipple as my mouth searches for hers again.

"Will you marry me?"

The words just slip out. I freeze, but she doesn't. I don't know if she heard me.

"Yes," she finally says.

I kiss her again and then pull away, looking straight into her eyes.

"What did you say?" I ask.

"I said yes." She smiles. "I'll marry you."

I kiss her again and again, pushing her down onto the couch and climbing on top of her. I had organized my thoughts into this big speech and written it down, but then...the question just came out.

"Wait a second." She laughs, sitting back up. "Aren't you supposed to have a ring for me?"

"I do!"

"You do?"

She is surprised, but I tell her to wait. I search the drawer in the console table by the foyer and find the box. Once it's in my hand, I get on one knee before her, open the box, and ask her again.

"Oh my God!" she whispers, covering her mouth with one hand. Her eyes get fixed on the ring and she doesn't answer.

"You're supposed to look at me, not the ring," I joke. She wraps her arms around me and whispers, "Yes, a million times yes," into my ear.

"I can't believe you got me this," Harley says, looking at the ring on her finger. "It's too big. Too opulent."

"It's perfect," I say.

"Yes, it is."

I tell her that I had it in my pocket on her

parents' wedding day and that my only regret was that I waited so long to ask her.

"It's okay," she reassures me.

"My only regret is that we're not married already."

"I love you," she whispers, placing her head on mine.

As we sit here in silence for a few moments, that's when I remember. This wasn't how it was supposed to go.

I was supposed to do this in front of the cameras. This was supposed to be a show.

Something that would raise Minetta's profile in the press. And now...we had this perfect moment and it's over. Or is it?

"What's wrong?" Harley asks.

"I have to tell you something."

I tell her everything about what Andrew Lindell asked me to do. Well, almost everything. She listens carefully and at first doesn't respond.

"So, were you really going to go through with it?"

"I didn't want to. And that's not why I asked. I've had that ring since your parents' wedding. That's the truth."

"I believe you," she whispers.

"I didn't bring this up to ruin our night, Harley. I brought this up because it's something that's weighing on me and I've promised myself that I won't be keeping any more secrets from you."

"So what do we do now?" she asks.

"I don't know."

"Do you think we should do it?" Harley asks after a moment of silence.

I shrug.

"What if he's right? What if this is the kind of storyline that will raise Minetta's profile in the media?"

"It will."

"So what happens then?"

"Well, hopefully more people will find out what we do and have a positive association with it and that will in turn raise the page views and the subscription rate."

"And what then?" she asks.

"His plan is to take the company public. That means that it will be traded on the open market. And all the initial investors are typically paid off handsomely in the process."

"Initial investors like him?"

"Yes."

"So, he wants to get out of the company? Not use it as a front for money laundering?"

"That's what I thought he was after before but I guess he has changed his mind. He wants to off-load Minetta and take his profits and leave."

"Wow," she whispers, surprised. I am surprised, too.

"Do you believe him?" she asks.

"About him wanting to take the company public?" I ask. She nods.

"It seems to be the only way that he will exit this deal with a lot more than he came into it with."

"Then let's do it," Harley says.

31

HARLEY

WHEN I SAY YES...

Sometimes you just have to decide to start living your life again even though you don't want to.

This is what I did when I lost my brother and this is what I had to do after losing my baby.

There's nothing else to do.

You have grieved and cried and spent days mourning.

And then...one day, you wake up and you know that you have to start doing something else again otherwise you might lose yourself in your grief completely.

That's why I said yes.

Jackson asked me to marry him while we were kissing on the couch.

His hand was up my shirt and our bodies were

touching for the first time since before that happened.

That moment felt so good. I forgot about my pain and everything that was wrong with my life, and instead I lost myself in the man I love.

And that's why when he asked me that question, that seemed to have taken him by surprise as well, I said yes.

There's a saying from a movie I saw a long time ago called Shawshank Redemption.

An innocent man finds himself in prison for life. It's unfair, and unjust, and horrible but he still has a decision to make.

His friend tells him in there, "You have to get busy living or get busy dying."

That's what I have to do, too. What happened was horrible, and unfair, and unjust but now it's up to me to live the rest of my life. I may not want to, but unless I get busy living, I will get busy dying.

So, I say yes. I say yes to Jackson. I say yes to hope. I say yes to life.

I AM DRESSED IN A GOWN, long and black. It is textured with little feathers lining the bottom.

It's hard to explain because I don't know much

about dresses or what they are made from, but I know how this one makes me feel.

I am a goddess.

This gown wraps around me in such a way that it makes me a vision.

My breasts are reaching for the heavens and when my breath quickens, they move up and down.

I am standing before a tall ship with enormous sails moving slightly in the breeze.

The boardwalk is empty except for the thousands of lights twinkling all around us, creating an atmosphere of romance and magic.

Jackson is standing before me, dressed in a tailored black tuxedo that hugs his every edge in just the right way.

It makes him look chiseled, and manly, and so sexy, it's everything I can do not to put my hands on him and rip it off right there.

His hair falls slightly into his face and he moves it out of the way.

As his hand graces his forehead, I detect a small tremble. His eyes dart away from mine for a second, his nervousness is apparent and disarming.

I squeeze his hand to convey to him that everything is going to be okay. He gives me a little smile out of the corner of his mouth. Neither of us has ever done anything like this, but it will be over soon.

"Harley," he says slowly. "I want to thank you. I want to thank you for being there for me through… everything that we have been through. As much as I loved you when we first fell in love, my love for you is so much more than that now and it's only growing every day."

These words are true, I can feel it in the pit of my stomach and shivers run down my spine.

"Harley Burke," Jackson says, getting down on one knee and opening the box. I glance down at the ring that I had worn around the house on my left finger for three full days and smile.

"Will you marry me?"

"Yes," I say with tears running down my cheeks. "A million times yes."

He places the ring on my finger and I pull him up to me. I put my lips onto his. He takes me into his arms and I know that everything is going to be okay.

32

HARLEY

WHEN I AM SURPRISED...

The cameras were there but it didn't feel like it.

Wherever they were, I didn't see them.

They were hidden as they were supposed to be and surprisingly the moment felt almost exactly like the first one.

Real.

True.

Honest.

"Thank you," Jackson says, back in our room at the house.

He is no longer wearing his tuxedo jacket and he's losing his collar.

I want to get out of this dress as well, but I also want to keep wearing it because of how amazing it makes me feel.

"You look...beautiful."

"Thank you, I hope the pictures and videos turn out good," I add.

"I'm sure they will."

He turns away from me. Something is still bothering him about this.

"You know you don't have to feel guilty. We got engaged. We are engaged. It's just not as romantic to show the first one. Not like it's possible at all anyway."

"I know." He shrugs.

"I love you," I whisper.

He puts his arms around me from the back, draping his head over my shoulder.

I bury my fingers in his hair for a bit and he gives off a little moan when I pull on it. Then I turn my head toward his.

Our lips collide.

A moment later, his hands are unzipping my dress and he is helping me out of it. My hands are pulling his shirt over his head and unbuckling his pants.

When we are completely free of our clothes, he walks me over to the bed and lowers himself on top of me.

"I've missed you," I whisper.

We haven't been intimate since before the

incident. I was always the one to pull away first, to put a brake on the situation.

But tonight, I feel different. This feels right.

"I missed you, too," he whispers. He kisses my neck, slowly making his way down my body. But then he stops.

"What's wrong?" I ask, looking down. "What?"

"What if we don't use protection?" Jackson says after a moment.

I stare at him, unsure as to how to respond. He pulls away from me, propping his head up on his hand and waits for me to answer.

"I...don't..." I start to say. Thoughts swirl around in my head as I try to focus my mind.

"I love you," he says forcefully and with confidence. "I love you and I want to have a baby with you. I am certain of it."

"You want to start...now?"

"Why not?"

"But it hasn't been enough time—"

"It hasn't? How long should we wait to do what we want?"

A smile forms at the corner of my mouth.

I know what he means.

Before I got pregnant, I also wasn't sure if I wanted a child. But now, I know that I do. So...why not?

"Okay," I say slowly.

He doesn't ask if I'm sure.

He just brings his lips to mine and pulls me back under him.

He is in control.

He puts his hands on my body, anywhere and everywhere and I love how this makes me feel.

A shiver of excitement rushes through me as he wraps me with his body. We should take this slow, but neither of us can.

His fingers bury themselves in my hair.

My fingers scratch against his back.

His mouth licks my neck.

Mine gasps for breath.

He makes his way down to my nipples. His kisses become more frantic.

Out of control.

My breathing speeds up to match his.

He is at my belly button and then below it. His tongue makes its way between my hip bones, where my panty line would be.

But instead of staying there, he goes even more south.

My legs open for him as he presses his mouth inside of me.

It plays with me, teases me, just before his fingers thrust inside.

Waves of passion overwhelm me and I grab onto the sheets to keep them at bay.

It's better when you don't give in right away, when you ride the ride of that wave for a little bit longer.

"I can't wait any longer," I whisper. "I need you in me."

My wish is his command.

He eases himself inside of me and suddenly our bodies become one.

We move as one.

We breathe as one.

We cling to each other as one.

A familiar feeling of warmth overwhelms my body.

He moves faster on top of me.

He yells my name.

I whisper his.

Afterward, we lie there for a few moments with our bodies still one.

"I love you," we say almost at the same time.

33

HARLEY

WHEN I GET CLOSER...

The following morning while Jackson is working and probably answering lots of questions about last night's surprise proposal, I sit down at my computer and continue to build a rapport with Parker as my online alter-ego Dani.

As Dani, I am his shy online friend, who doesn't want to video chat but is okay with sharing other things about her life, including pictures of my body.

No nude pictures, of course, but I do send a few sexy shots holding a sign with a saying that he requested.

He wants proof that I'm not an old fat man and I'm only happy to comply.

Over the last few weeks, we have built quite a

friendship actually. We talk almost every day and for a long time as well.

The nauseating feeling that I got when I first started talking to him has almost vanished and it's now easier for me to forget who I am actually online with.

That's the thing about texting, isn't it?

It removes you so far from the person that you can just fill in the blanks with someone else entirely.

A few days ago, I learned that he grew up with his mom who worked all the time as an overnight nurse and then spent her days nagging him (his words, of course).

Today, we also talk about how overbearing and demanding she is, and in order to show him that I understand where he's coming from, I tell him about my parents and how they have always preferred my sister to me.

I complain to him about how perfect she is and how she always got straight As and never did anything wrong, while I could never do anything right.

This resonates with him and he quickly jumps to my side by cursing them out and then adding 'no offense' at the end.

No worries, I type. *They deserve it.*

Of course they do, he adds.

When there's a little bit of a lull in the conversation, I decide to finally go for it.

So I was thinking...

Yeah?

What if we meet up?

He doesn't respond at first, but I wait.

Don't you want to video chat first?

No. I want our first time seeing each other to be in real life.

He doesn't respond at first, and I freeze thinking that I've taken it too far.

The thing is that there's something that I didn't tell you before.

What?

I don't know if I should tell you.

You can trust me, I reassure him with a smiling emoji.

I'm in trouble.

What kind of trouble?

I'm actually running from the law a bit right now. So, I have to be careful.

I don't respond for a bit, just to make him nervous.

Dani? Are you there?

So...are you telling me you're an outlaw? I ask coyly.

Yes.

That's kind of...sexy, I type, wanting to throw up.

You're crazy LOL.

Only a little bit. So what did you do?

I took things a bit too far with my ex-girlfriend, he lies.

What do you mean?

She broke things off with me real suddenly so I was stalking her a bit. But nothing bad.

I sit back in my chair, shaking my head. Is this what he really thinks or are these the lies that he tells himself just to get through the day? But I have to role-play.

So you stalked her online?

Yes. And a little bit in real life. Then she pressed charges when I tried to talk her. I wanted to make things right but she just freaked out. You know how girls can be.

I hope you're not still into her, I say, ignoring his misogynistic comment.

Not at all.

I don't believe you.

Well, you have to, he types quickly. *I don't. I know it was wrong for me to follow her. Besides she's a total bitch. Nothing like you. Now, I just want to be with you.*

You promise?

Yes, of course.

Good.

I stare at the screen for a moment, knowing very well that this is the tipping point. This is the moment that I won't be able to take back. Then I put my hands back on the keyboard and type,

Where do you want to meet up?

He says that he has to think about it for a while and I give him the space.

He pivots the conversation more to my day and I make up some mundane problems to keep him entertained.

The only way this is going to work is if I can get him to trust me. I know that and that's why I'm doing this in the first place.

Perhaps there are some more technical ways to get this done but I'm not a private investigator. The police and the FBI are useless, so this is all I have.

My computer dings and another message shows up on the screen. This one is from Sam.

Yes, that Sam.

Parker wasn't the only one who hurt me that night, so he will not be the only one who will pay for what he did.

Once I found out and confirmed that I am talking to the right Sam Davis, I started to become his friend as well.

And then more than a friend. We flirt and he

keeps trying to take it further than Parker ever suggests.

I feel like Sam wants me to be more playful so that's what I am. I send him pictures as well, but I refuse to do a video chat.

He is more resistant than Parker.

Probably because he isn't hiding. There were a few of our conversations that I thought that I had almost lost him.

He got mad that I wouldn't video chat and said I was a fake.

It took more than a few pictures in a bra and panties holding random objects that he named for me to convince him that I was still a good looking girl.

Where do you want to meet? I write.

Tomorrow afternoon. 1524 Atlantic Avenue.

My heart jumps into my throat. I don't expect for him to agree to it so quickly.

Unless you want to meet somewhere more public?
He writes.

Where is this? I ask

My place.

A million scenarios run through my mind at the same time.

Somewhere more public would be safer, but that's not what I want. His place is actually perfect.

He doesn't live with anyone else.

It's an apartment and it's in a large building but at least it's not out in the open.

Sam is free. He has nothing to be afraid of.

But I do. Especially, if this goes the way I think it might.

Your place is perfect, I type.

34

HARLEY

WHEN I GO TO MEET HIM...

The following morning arrives much sooner than I want it to. I still don't have much of a plan.

What do I do?

How do I protect myself?

And what is my end game anyway?

I want to make Sam pay for what he did, but how? As I sit in the back of the taxi, my thoughts go in circles.

I remember everything that he did to me. I remember how scared he was yet how forceful. I remember how much he hurt me by leaving me there after his fight with Parker.

All of these memories come to me at once and I can barely get out of the car on my own.

I still have a lot of time before our meeting, so I duck into the coffee shop around the corner.

I had the driver drop me off a few blocks away so that no one could follow me here.

But what other reason would I have to be in this part of Queens? It's not exactly nice or scenic. I don't think anyone really comes here besides those who live here.

In the coffee shop, I get an espresso and nurse it by the window. I stand out. I don't belong.

I can see people staring.

Will they remember my face after they showed it on the news? This is a terrible idea. I know that already.

I have no plan except to talk to him. But I don't need privacy for that, right? It would be better to talk in public.

I'm just afraid that he won't be honest in public.

So that's why I'm here with this stupid gun in my purse. It's loaded. I run my fingers over the outside, feeling its contours through the fabric.

The gun is unlicensed and unregistered.

I got it the same day I started talking to Parker online. Armslist is a website devoted specifically to private sales of guns and other weapons related gear.

The guy who sold it to me didn't ask any questions or even for my name.

I wore a hoodie over my black wig and disguised my face with heavy makeup so that he would have a harder time identifying me.

When he asked why I needed a gun, I told him that I was getting it for protection. That part was true. Sort of.

I walk up to Sam's building and look it up and down. There is garbage all over the place and the outside is peeling and old.

This place is the definition of the projects, along with a bunch of teenage boys in oversized clothing standing outside.

They whistle at me as I walk by, so I flip them off. I immediately regret calling attention to myself and quickly duck into the open foyer, hoping that my disguise is enough for them to forget me.

I debate waiting for the elevator but then decide to just climb the stairs.

His apartment is only on the seventh floor and the last thing I want to do is to be stuck in the elevator with someone with a particularly good memory for faces.

Luckily, the staircase is empty all the way to his floor and I don't see a soul. I take a few moments to catch my breath on the landing before opening the door and going inside the long narrow hallway.

More peeling paint welcomes me along with an unforgettable scent of urine. What the hell? Why pee in your own hallway? I wonder to myself silently, burying my nose in my arm.

"NYPD! Open up!" someone yells. A loud bang startles me, making me jump against the wall. Peeking around the corner, I see five or so police officers all dressed in protective gear rush through the door of an apartment. I can't be sure if it's the one that belongs to Sam so I count the doors and try to line up the numbers in my head.

No, it's not his, I decide. Then count them again.

No, it has to be.

A few neighbors peek their heads out, but the cops crowding around the door tell them to get back inside.

I stay put as well.

I want to leave.

I should.

But I can't bring myself to do it until I see him with my own two eyes.

I look down at my phone. It has been almost five minutes. Then ten. Okay. I guess I should go, I decide.

But then, just as I'm about to leave, they emerge.

The cops are crowding around him, two are holding his handcuffed arms behind his back.

His head is hanging down.

They are about to turn down my hallway.

I back away slowly, and then turn around and run.

They are going to take the elevator and I need to disappear into the staircase before they see me.

"What the hell are *you* doing here?" Sam asks. His voice carries all the way down the hallway. I freeze.

"Nothing," I mumble.

"You've got to be kidding me! Is this what it's about? This stupid cunt?"

The cops shake their heads, clearly surprised by my presence but trying not to let him in on it.

"I have no idea what he's talking about," I say and open the door to the staircase. But someone stops me.

"Wait a second! Are you Dani?" Sam has a lightbulb moment.

My body stops, freezes, as if I were a deer who sees headlights in the middle of a dark empty road.

They pull him away into the elevator but another cop, dressed in a leather jacket, corners me.

He asks me questions that I don't know how to answer. Finally, something occurs to me.

I have to tell him the closest thing I can to the truth. That's the only way he'll believe me.

"Okay, fine, I'll tell you who I am," I start. "I'm

his ex-girlfriend. I made up a fake profile online using the name Dani. I wanted to talk to him. To see if he was talking to any other girls. That's all. We had a plan to meet today before you busted in there."

35

HARLEY

WHEN I GO TO MEET HIM...

I can't really tell if the detective believes me or not.

I'm not sure what to do and the silence makes me really unconformable so I repeat what I just said.

Meanwhile, my thoughts return to my purse.

If he were to search my bag then he will find an unlicensed, unregistered, and untraceable gun.

Please, please, I say silently to myself. Please don't let him search my bag.

"So what's your real name?" he asks, taking out a pen and paper. For a moment I consider telling him the truth but then I lie.

"Susan Shafer," I say quickly. He asks to see my identification but I tell him that I don't have it with me. He asks for my number and luckily, I tell him my real one. When he calls it, my phone goes off.

"Okay, Susan Shafer. I'll be in touch."

I give him a little unassuming nod.

After we ride down the elevator together in silence, he turns to me and says, "You look like a really pretty girl underneath all of that garbage you have on your face. You deserve someone a lot better than that asshole. I hope you know that."

"I do," I whisper.

"If you ever want to get a drink, call me," he says, handing me his card.

I am so overwhelmed by everything that just happened that the last thing that I expect is a proposition for a date.

"Are you allowed to date ex-girlfriends of people you arrest?"

"Nope." He winks at me and walks away.

As soon as he disappears out of sight, I run to the nearest trash can and throw up.

I WALK a few blocks away from Sam's house and then call a ride share company. A Prius shows up almost immediately and after checking to see that the driver is who the app says he should be, I get in.

Usually, I make small talk but this time I can't bring myself to say a word.

The driver doesn't seem to care and turns up the volume on the radio.

My phone rings in my hand.

It's Julie.

I actually have to look at the name for a few rings just to believe my eyes. I haven't talked to her since our fight.

I called and texted her a bunch of times but she never got back to me until today.

I'm tempted to let the call go to voice mail but since I haven't spoken to her in a while I pick up.

"Will you come over?" she asks without even bothering with hello.

"Yes," I say immediately and tell the driver her address.

When I ring her doorbell, she buzzes me in almost immediately and then throws her arms around my neck when I knock on her door.

She cries and I cry along with her. I've missed her, too, and it wasn't until what just happened at Sam's that I realized exactly how much.

I love Jackson and I want to marry him, but Julie is my best girlfriend.

I love and need her in a completely different way than I love and need Jackson.

"I'm really sorry about everything," she mumbles through her tears.

"It's okay, really," I reassure her over and over again.

She invites me inside and we climb onto her bed to talk, just like we used to when we were roommates. I take off my shoes and she brings us our teas with lemon-custard cookies.

"Wow, you've prepared," I joke, biting into it and letting myself enjoy its deliciousness.

"Thanks for coming," she mumbles, swallowing her cookie almost whole.

We sit and talk about nothing in particular at first, just to get to know about each other's lives again.

We are both avoiding the one thing that perhaps we should be talking about, but it's okay for now. It's nice just to be here. It's nice just to talk to her again.

After three cups of tea, we are finally secure enough in our newfound friendship to broach the subject again.

"I'm so sorry about your loss," I say.

"Thank you," Julie says, hanging her head. I can see the pain on her face even though she is averting her eyes. She doesn't want me to see that she's crying but a rogue tear breaks free, betraying her.

"And I'm so sorry for your loss as well," she says after a moment. "Your...baby."

"Yeah," I whisper.

I reach out to her, pulling her close to me. We hold each other for some time without letting go.

"I just really want him dead."

"Who?"

"Their killer."

All I can do is nod in agreement.

She asks me if I know of anything else or if the police know anything.

I really want to tell her that I'm talking to Parker online and about my whole plan, and I have to bite my tongue to stop myself.

I can't bring her into this. I can't put myself in danger like that. Besides, what if she were to do something to stop me? No, no one can know.

"They don't know anything," I say with a shrug.

"What about Jackson?"

"What about him?"

"Is he going to hire a private investigator?"

"I don't know. We haven't talked about it."

"Well, the more time that passes the less likely this thing will ever be solved. After the first forty-eight hours..."

Her words trail off. I know how to finish her thought.

Everyone knows that the police solve the

majority of the crimes within this timeframe and after that things get a lot more difficult.

Clues and witnesses disappear.

"I am sure that they are doing their best," I say through my teeth. I regret it immediately. Her eyes dart up to my face and narrow.

"What are you talking about? You don't have any faith in the police!"

"No, that's not what I meant," I backtrack.

"Yes, it is," she says, taking my hands into hers. "Tell me. What's going on?"

The answer is at the tip of my tongue. But I force myself to stay quiet. No, I will not put myself in danger or her in the position to keep quiet in return for one moment of relief.

"Julie, I really don't know anything. I was just... trying to comfort you. That's all."

"So, Jackson isn't going to hire a private investigator?" She looks up at me. This is what she wants to hear. This will give her momentary peace. So why not lie?

"Yes, okay? I wasn't supposed to tell anyone but he is looking into hiring someone."

A big wide smile comes over her face and she pulls me close to her in a big hug. "I knew it," she whispers into my ear. "I just knew it."

36

JACKSON

WHEN I MEET UP WITH HIM...

After the staged proposal, Minetta Media is overwhelmed with positive press.

There are pictures of Harley and me in all the online magazines and even in some of the tabloids.

That's a big deal since I'm not technically a particularly well known person outside of the business world.

Understandably, Andrew Lindell is pleased with the results and now wants to take it a step further.

He wants us to get married and give him access to all of the proceedings.

The details of the wedding are up to us, of course, and he will provide us with an emergency wedding planner who can make miracles happen no matter how big of a wedding we want to have.

The proposal doesn't feel like a fake to me since I did propose to Harley earlier for real, so I'm not entirely sure about going forward with this.

Besides, he didn't exactly live up to his end of the bargain by telling me where I could find Parker.

"You will know as soon as you get married. That I promise you," he tells me over another tense lunch, ones that I have learned to dread.

"You said that last time," I point out.

"I know and apologize for that. I can pay you for it instead? But this is the only kind of leverage I have at this point."

"Why is this so important to you?" I ask.

"I want out of this business. And you want me out of this business, right? So why don't you just do what I ask? You want to marry. You are going to have a videographer and a photographer anyway. So...who is getting hurt here? You are the one who will have the whole wedding paid for."

"I may not be worth as much as I was before, but I assure you, I can pay for my own wedding."

"Of course," he says. "I didn't mean to offend you. But you have to know where I am coming from. I need this company to go public in the best way. That's the only way I can exit it and make myself some money."

"Please don't take this as an offense, but I

thought you wanted Minetta as a way to launder money."

He smiles and sits back in his seat.

"Hypothetically, of course," I add just in case anyone is listening or recording this conversation.

"I did."

"And now?"

"Now, not so much. I see that I can buy something a little bit less valuable to do that, if I want to do that. Hypothetically speaking, of course."

LATER THAT AFTERNOON, I tell Harley what happened at lunch. Much to my surprise, she likes the idea.

I thought that she would put up more of a fight but her mind is elsewhere. In fact, she barely cares at all.

I have no idea what's bothering her, so I put it to one side and decide to bring it up later. Much to my surprise, she actually broaches the subject first.

"Sorry I was so distracted before. I was thinking about it and why not do it?"

"I don't know," I agree.

"This will go a long way to getting him out of Minetta's business, right?"

I nod.

"So, let's do it. We are going to get married anyway. We can do it on Lindell's dime."

"He wants to do it within a month."

"Can we do it in two weeks?" she asks. I take a step back.

"You don't want to marry me in two weeks?" Harley jokes.

"No...but still, isn't that too soon?"

"What's another two weeks?" she asks, shrugging. She's right of course. I know that. But something still makes me uncomfortable. Why is she so into this idea?

"Can I ask you something?"

Harley nods. Her eyes twinkle in the falling light.

"Did Lindell talk to you about this?"

"No."

"Are you sure?"

"Of course."

I give her a peck on the cheek and accept her answer.

Still, something doesn't feel right.

It's like she is hiding something.

But until I know what it is, I don't want to press her. Neither of us are back to normal yet.

Besides...I am hiding something, too.

I haven't told Harley the one thing that Andrew

keeps promising me in exchange for all of these theatrics.

It's the only reason I am doing any of this, and it's the thing that he is still holding out on.

I've debated whether I should tell Harley about Andrew's promise. On one hand, she deserves to know.

On the other, the thing that I plan to do with that information is nothing that she should know anything about.

I don't worry about her betraying me to the police. I know that she won't talk to them.

But I don't want to put her in danger.

She has suffered enough.

If she were to know his whereabouts, there is no way that she would let me go by myself to confront him.

If I tried to stop her, then she would follow me.

Worrying about her is not something I can do when I am confronting a man like Parker Huntington. No, this is for me to take care of. He is mine to eliminate on my own.

37

HARLEY

WHEN HE TELLS ME...

Andrew Lindell wants to give us a big wedding.

He wants to plan it and pay for it and in exchange for that he will sell the video and photo rights to magazines and then possibly give Jackson back his company after it goes public.

Jackson seems to be very concerned with this whole situation, but I frankly don't see what the big deal is.

I want to marry Jackson.

The sooner the better.

I don't want to plan anything but I do want it to be gorgeous and amazing and perfect.

I've never been much into parties, but I have looked through a few bridal magazines.

Everything is so staged and perfect and there

have been more than a few pages that I earmarked for the fabulous occasion.

But as for going over all the details of the event planning?

No, that's not for me.

I can't even pretend to have an interest in that. Jackson isn't so sure about the whole process.

"Look, we wouldn't really plan every aspect of this event ourselves anyway, right?" I ask.

"What do you mean?"

"Well, if we were to get married in say a year? If we took the proper amount of time to make all the preparations. That doesn't mean that we would actually make all the preparations. You would probably insist on hiring a wedding planner who showed us pre-selected options that we would either approve or disapprove of."

"Yes, I guess." Jackson nods.

"So, how is this any different? It's just more work for the wedding planner if we do it sooner."

The more we talk, the more comfortable Jackson seems to get with the idea. Neither of us really wants to wait to get married and neither of us have really high expectations of what kind of wedding we should have.

While Jackson excuses himself to make the call to Andrew and confirm our plan to wed in two weeks, I check my phone.

I sign into my other Facebook account to see if there are any messages from Parker or Sam.

There aren't any.

I don't expect any from Sam, given that he's in jail now, but I am worried about one thing.

What if Sam reached out to Parker and told him that I had pretended to be someone online?

Maybe that's why Parker isn't replying to any of my messages.

I write a casual *miss you* and send it hoping that this one gets a reply. But it doesn't.

Shit.

I really messed up.

I shouldn't have met up with Sam. He wasn't really the one I was after. And now, it's all ruined. Parker knows about me and there's no way that I'll ever find him again.

When Jackson comes back and tells me that everything is set with our wedding, he wraps his arms around me and I let my worries disappear. I can't do anything about Parker not writing me back, but I can put him out of my mind, at least for a few moments.

I lose myself in the moment and his mouth.

When our mouths touch, I feel the urgency that has been building up within me. I am hungry for him. It has been way too long since I've felt his strong body on top of mine, and yet this feels like it's our first time.

I take a deep breath. He smells like home. This is where I belong.

I want to take it slowly, but my body is more in charge than I am. My hands are moving up and down his back, fingers digging into his skin. When he tries to pull away even for a second, I pull him closer.

He's on top of me. Our breathing becomes one. His body grinds against mine for a few moments. Then I open my legs under him and welcome him inside.

We moan simultaneously. When I open my eyes, I see the muscles in his arms tense and relax with each thrust. I press my nose to his right bicep, inhaling his scent.

The end is not so much a wave, but a tsunami. It overwhelms my senses. It makes me scream his name. It makes my legs go numb.

AFTERWARD, Jackson has to take care of some work thing on his computer. I decide to spend the rest of the day in bed watching Netflix. On the second episode of *Grey's Anatomy*, my phone dings. It's Parker.

Let's meet up now.

As I stare at the message, my hands turn to ice. Why does he want to meet now? What does he know? Does he know anything?

I don't know if I can, I type, my fingers shaking.

It's now or never.

What's going on?

I can't tell you over this. Just meet me in Montauk. I'll text you the address once you're on your way.

What are you doing there?

Montauk is a small town on the tip of Long Island. There's only one way in and one way out by car as it's completely isolated by water. You'd think that it's hardly the perfect place for a fugitive to hide out. But maybe that's why he was there in the first place. While the authorities have checkpoints set up on the border with Canada, he's hiding in Montauk.

I'll tell you everything once you get here.

I don't think I can go now.

Dani, it's now or never. You have 4 hours.

What's going to happen then?

I'm getting on a boat and I'm getting the hell out of America.

I don't have much time to decide. It's about a three hour drive all the way there and that's if there's no traffic.

I'll see you in three hours, I type.

38

JACKSON

WHEN I FIND OUT...

W hile in a meeting with the higher ups at Minetta, I am supposed to be listening to the reports and findings about our progress but my thoughts are on Harley.

I miss her even though I just saw her less than two hours ago.

Is this normal? Probably not.

But it feels good to care about someone so much again. I just want to spend all of my time with her.

I want to take her into my arms and do absolutely nothing for a long time except be with her.

Nowadays, a honeymoon is typically a week long but I want to take a month off to be with her.

Maybe even more if I can arrange everything just right.

We haven't talked about that yet, but I am thinking of leasing a one hundred foot yacht and going down to the Virgin Islands or St. Barts, somewhere in the Caribbean, and just leaving all of our problems on land.

My phone vibrates and I discretely look at the screen, expecting it to be a text from Harley.

But it's actually Julie.

They just made up and while I'm stuck in this meeting, Harley went over to her place. It's unusual for Julie to call me, so I excuse myself and pick up.

"Hey, are you seriously getting married in two weeks?" Julie starts the conversation as if we are already in the middle of one.

"Yeah, why?"

"I just know of this perfect little place that I think Harley would love."

"Okay," I say slowly. "Why don't you tell her about it then?"

"I would but she's not picking up the phone."

My heart sinks.

"Wait, what?" I ask, certain that I just didn't hear her right.

"I just wanted to tell someone. Working on this wedding will really take my mind off things—" Julie starts to say but I cut her off.

"What do you mean, not picking up? Isn't she with you?"

There's silence on the other end.

"She's not with you?" I bark.

"No…" she says slowly.

"She said she was going to your place," I say, putting the phone on speaker. I click on the app store and download the Find my iPhone app. I know that iPhones can be tracked remotely. I wait for it to load and then stare at the screen for a few moments to process what I'm seeing.

"What is she doing in Long Island?" I ask Julie.

"I have no idea."

"Something's wrong," I mumble to myself. "Okay, I have to go."

"Where?"

"Long Island."

Everyone in the room stares at me with looks of concern and disbelief.

"I have to go," I say, grabbing my phone, laptop, and car keys.

Once I'm on my way with the GPS giving me directions to her location, I call Andrew Lindell.

"Where's Parker?" I demand to know.

"What is going on? Are you okay?"

"I don't have time to explain. But I think Harley is about to meet up with him."

"No, that's impossible," he says under his breath.

"She lied to me about where she's going. And she has been acting weird for a bit, closing her laptop as soon as I walk into the room."

"She could be seeing another guy," he suggests. If we weren't on the phone, I'd probably clock him. But I also know that he's right. If I'm lucky, then she is just meeting up with a guy.

"That's why you have to tell me where Parker is. Then I'll know if she's headed to see him or not," I say sternly.

"Okay, fine, let me see what I can find out. I'll call you back."

I drive what feels like hours before he calls me back. The city disappears and a slew of small towns and suburbs dot the highway. The vegetation is lush and green, and the clouds all around are menacing, threatening a downpour.

"My source says that he's in Long Island," Andrew says.

I clench my jaw. She is not out there for a date. She knows where he is and she's going to meet up with him.

"Jackson, did you hear me?"

"Yes," I finally say. "That's where she's headed."

"Shit," Andrew whispers. "But you know Long Island is a big place. Where is she exactly?"

I look at her location. It hasn't changed in half an hour.

"Montauk."

"That's where Parker is," he says quietly.

Andrew offers to call the police, but I can call them just as easily as he can.

The problem is that I have no idea why Harley is going there. She must have some sort of plan.

She kept it from me and she's doing all of this completely below the radar, so calling the cops might put her in danger.

If she is going there to kill him, which is quite likely, then the last thing I want is to turn her over to the police.

The authorities have no idea where Parker is, otherwise, he'd be arrested.

So maybe letting her carry out her plan isn't the worst idea.

But then again, what if something happens?

What if she doesn't really have a plan?

Then what?

Then she is alone with a man, a murderer, who will do anything to hurt her.

39

HARLEY

WHEN I SEE HIM...

The address that Parker gives me belongs to a mobile home park. There are people sitting on steps and grilling burgers outside.

I sit just outside of it, in Jackson's car, trying to figure out what to do. If I walk right down the main road everyone will see me.

And what is about to happen is not something anyone should see.

I look around for a better option.

It's the last single wide mobile home on the right side, backing into the woods. The trees are thick and green and it's difficult to see a thing through them.

I get out of the car and make my way through the woods. The gun that I took to Sam's house is in the pocket of my hoodie.

I run my finger over the barrel and wonder if I will have the strength to shoot him if the time comes.

I didn't have a plan when I first started driving but I do now. I am not going to shoot him. It probably looks that way, but that's not what I'm here for. I got the gun for my protection.

Parker is too good to be executed with just a bullet to the head.

No, he deserves to suffer a long sentence in a maximum security prison where he would sit in a cell twenty-three hours a day.

Through the trees, I see him in the kitchen of his mobile home.

I dial the police and when the operator answers, I whisper for them to come quick and give them the address of this place.

"What's going on?" she asks after dispatching officers.

"There's a fugitive who committed a murder here."

"Don't do anything until they arrive," she warns me but I hang up.

I don't have any plans to do anything except to have a little chat.

I knock on the door.

"Dani!" I hear him say. When he sees me, he

pushes the door back in my face. I put my foot out to stop it from slamming shut.

"Sit down!" I pull the gun from my pocket and point it at him.

"Stop moving and sit down!" I say sternly. This time he listens.

I can tell that he is both nervous and happy to see me. He is getting a sick thrill from this, but so am I.

For the first time, I feel like I'm in control. For the first time, he is the one who is afraid.

"So...wait a second, you are Dani?" he asks, taking a seat on the couch.

I close the door behind me without turning around and then position myself right in front of it.

My feet spread apart, my hands are wrapped firmly around the gun. I've shot a gun only at a gun range, never pointing it at a living thing.

I am no expert, but I know that it's important to maintain a bit of a distance and to have both hands around the barrel for stabilization.

"How did you find me?"

"You weren't hard to find. I just never looked before."

"Fake profile, huh? I never expected that. You got me there."

He is oozing with confidence.

For some reason, he is proud of the fact that he made me chase him for once.

Instead of focusing on an empty stare, I try to remember all of the millions of things that I wanted to ask him. But my mind goes blank.

"So, what do you want?" Parker finally asks. "You got me here, cornered me. What are you going to do now? Kill me?"

"Maybe."

"You wouldn't."

"Don't tempt me."

Luckily, he doesn't. I want to check how long it has been since I called the police but I can't let him know that I'm waiting for something. What I know is that we probably don't have much time.

"Why?" I finally ask. "Why have you been so obsessed with me all this time?"

He doesn't answer right away. "I don't know," he finally says. "When I started reading your blog, it was all so real. I had to find out who you really were."

"But you did and you found out that I made all of that up."

"So?"

"So? Why wasn't that enough? Why did you keep...following me?"

He darts his eyes to the floor, avoiding eye

contact with me. Finally, when he gathers enough strength, he looks at me again.

"I thought that maybe I could make you fall in love with me," he says. The look on his face resembles the gaze of a lost child. I almost feel sorry for him. *Almost.*

"So, why did you kill Martin?" I ask.

"Who is Martin?"

"My bodyguard. The man you executed on your bike. Did you forget that already?"

He laughs, and the sad look vanishes. Instead, the psychopath underneath emerges. I'm taken aback by how quickly he undergoes the change.

"How did you know it was me?"

"Of course, it was you. Who else could it be?"

He laughs again.

"Okay, fine," he admits it. "I'll tell you the truth."

Just at that moment, the front door swings open.

40

HARLEY

WHEN I'M STARTLED…

I t takes me a moment to realize who is standing behind me. But in turning around, I make a terrible mistake.

You should never turn your body away from the man you are pointing the gun at. Once I do, Parker collides with me.

He pulls me down to the floor and then immediately reaches over me.

My eyes follow his arm, and I grab onto him just before he grabs the gun.

Jackson kicks the gun away from him and then punches him in the face. Once. Twice. And then over and over again as I get up to my feet.

"Stop! Stop!"

"No, I'm going to kill this asshole."

"Stop, it's not worth it!" I scream. "The cops are coming."

And with that, cars with loud sirens pull up to the mobile home, nearly deafening me with their cacophony of sound.

When I pull Jackson off Parker, his hand is a bloody mess but not as much as Parker's face.

It's barely recognizable.

Fear starts to build up within me.

What have I done?

Jackson is here because of me and now they are going to arrest him for killing this asshole. Jackson's life is going to be ruined, and it's all my fault.

THE REST of the day is a series of moments, and together just a blur.

Luckily, the paramedics get there in time to revive Parker and take him to the hospital.

He may still die there, but so far, he's alive and under arrest.

The Montauk police separate us and ask me a million questions about my intentions. I assume that they are doing the same thing with Jackson.

I decide to tell them the truth.

I tell them every last bit of the truth and hope that Jackson does the same.

I don't know what Jackson knows, but I had no intentions of killing him, or even shooting him.

That's why I called them for help.

"I just wanted to talk to him, that's all. This has been going on for a very long time and I wanted a few minutes to talk to him. But I called you and asked you to come because I knew that I would need help," I tell them.

"And your boyfriend?"

"I had no idea that he was going to show up. I didn't tell anyone where I was going."

They aren't entirely satisfied with my story and they keep bringing in new investigators to ask me more questions.

I answer them to the best of my ability, repeating the truth every time.

Once they are all out of officers, detectives from NYPD show up along with the FBI.

Now, it's their turn to ask me questions and I comply. I answer all of them and later that night, they finally let me go.

I don't know if things would've turned out this way if I hadn't decided to record my entire conversation with Parker on my phone.

But on the spur of the moment, I downloaded

the recording app and dropped the phone into my crossover bag.

Luckily, the recording ended up being quite a good quality and they heard what happened during the whole scene.

When I walk out in the main hallway, near the entrance of the police station, I see Jackson.

He runs over to me and takes me into his arms. Finally, I let out a big sigh of relief.

"It's over. It's finally over," he whispers.

41

HARLEY

AFTERWARD...

We marry two weeks later in a small intimate ceremony at the venue that Julie found for us.

It's a small little bookstore specializing in independently published romance novels, thrillers, and other fiction.

The bookstore is quaint and cute, with large stainless windows which let in a mosaic of light.

But the really beautiful spot is the garden.

I walk down an alleyway of cobblestones, surrounded by walls covered in ivy.

Large rosebushes grow all around the walls and our guests sit in ivory white chairs right in front of the gazebo where Jackson stands waiting for me.

I am dressed in a tight fitting antique white

dress that hugs my figure and is scattered with the light of a thousand sequins.

The gown is shoulder-baring making me feel like an elegant and glamorous princess.

The look on Jackson's face tells me that I chose the right dress.

We do not write our own vows but instead repeat the vows that the officiant says.

But then as we are walking down the aisle, married and holding hands, he looks at me and says, "I feel like I have been your husband forever. It's as if we have always been married throughout our time in all the world."

Goose bumps run down my arms. I know exactly what he means.

"It's as if our souls had been united long before this moment," I add. He gives me another kiss and everyone claps excitedly.

AFTER THE WEDDING, Andrew Lindell and his people release pictures and videos of our ceremony and we are celebrated in both print and online magazines for having a small intimate and affordable wedding even though we could've spent a million dollars on it.

At first, I thought that I wanted to have a big

lavish wedding, but when the wedding planner showed up with her group of ten assistants, I got overwhelmed with all the decisions and instead reached out to Julie for help.

Jackson was onboard with whatever so we went with this small venue and a limited number of guests.

Only twenty-five close family and friends made the cut and that was more than enough.

These were the people who meant the world to us and it was amazing having them there to celebrate our love.

The one person Jackson didn't want to invite was Aurora, but I insisted on it.

She played a big role in our relationship, even if I didn't want her to at first, and she was a good friend to Jackson throughout a lot of difficulties in his life.

I was expecting her to show up with a new boyfriend, but she surprised me. She came alone.

When I asked her about Elliot Woodward, she said that was the final straw. After they broke up, he was arrested for raping his personal assistant, and that's when she knew that she couldn't go on with her life like she was before.

Otherwise, it would end in shambles.

So, now she is taking time off from men for a long while in order to focus on herself.

She has even booked tickets to a wellness retreat to Thailand where she will sit in silent meditation for a week.

Later that evening, Jackson pulls me aside to share more good news.

His private investigator called and said that Sam was arrested in a big drug bust and for second-degree murder of an associate and was facing more than thirty years.

Parker would stand trial for first degree murder along with kidnapping and a slew of other charges.

Both of them were denied bail as they are awaiting trial and the prosecutor's office was certain that they were both going to get a lot of time.

I wrap my arms around his neck and kiss him passionately on his lips.

"So, what are we waiting for?" I ask, pulling him back to the dance floor. "Let's celebrate!"

42

HARLEY

A NEW BEGINNING...

The glass smells like most windows at any airport, musty yet clean with the strong scent of a pine cleaning product. But that's where the comparisons stop. Unlike the gates at JFK, filled with blitzed travelers overloaded with too many bags, we are the only ones here.

His private jet, Gulfstream G550, with its beige leather interior offering large overstuffed reclining seats that look like they belong in an upscale movie theater, is having technical difficulties. The staff and crew are more than apologetic, often checking on us in the terminal while we wait.

The terminal is only a terminal in name. In reality, it's more like the lobby of the Four Seasons. Tufted leather couches with matching chairs, an elegant fireplace, and a polished grand piano that I wish I could play. When one of the staff sees me watching a video on my phone, he tells us about their private movie theater with eight rocking recliners and a selection of new releases only available in theaters.

"Why even get on the plane?" I joke. "We should just spend our honeymoon here."

Jackson laughs. I can see that he is very at ease with all of this luxury, but I'm still not. Maybe I'll never be and that's okay. All of this is beautiful and grand, but I think it's important to remember what life was like before. And what life is like for most people out there.

Jackson looks away somewhere over the horizon. He is here but also not here.

"Are you okay?" I ask. It takes him a moment to answer. I am not surprised. He just heard the news this morning.

Lindell's plan has worked out. Minetta is going public and he will be more than tripling his investment after the deal goes through.

"I'm more than okay," he says. "I'm just still a little dazed over how all of this turned out."

"Yeah, it's pretty great," I say. "Now that Lindell will be out of your hair, what do you think you want to do?"

"I'm going to take some time off," he says without a beat.

"Really?" I ask.

"We made a lot of money off this deal. A lot more than I ever could've dreamed of. And I think I deserve a break. A really, really long break."

This makes me smile. This time off means that we will have all of our time to ourselves. That's what I want more than anything.

"So, where are we going exactly?" I ask. I know that it's somewhere sunny and warm, and in the Caribbean but I don't know where exactly.

"It's a surprise," Jackson says, his eyes smoldering.

"I know, but I don't know now. And I'll be surprised for sure."

He shakes his head, looking at the time on his watch.

"How long has it been?" I ask.

"Almost two hours."

Just then one of our flight attendants approaches us and says that they are finishing up and we'll be taking off in about twenty minutes.

"Okay, now you have to tell me!" I turn to Jackson. He shakes his head again, pursing his lips.

"Are you really not going to tell me?" I ask. "Okay, fine. Then I won't tell you my surprise either."

"You have a surprise, too?"

"Yep. And I thought I would tell you now, but if you're going to be this difficult then you'll have to wait."

He smiles, pulling me out of my seat and into his lap. Our eyes focus on each other's for a moment.

"We are going to the Caribbean and then wherever you want," he says slowly.

I don't understand.

"I got a boat. One-hundred foot yacht, just for us. We are flying into St. Barts and then we can go anywhere you want for however long you want."

"Thailand?" I jokingly challenge him.

"We can go to Thailand." He nods, kissing me.

"That will be a long trip."

"We have the rest of our lives."

I kiss him. Kissing me back, he buries his hands in my hair, pulling me even closer to him.

"Okay, my turn!" I whisper through our interlocked lips. I reach for my purse and fish around it for a moment trying to find it.

When I show him the little plastic stick with the word 'pregnant' on it, his eyes light up.

"Seriously?" A wide smile settles on his mouth as he looks at the word and then at me and then back at the screen.

"Yes," I whisper. "We are going to have a baby."

"I love you. I love you so much."

"I love you, too."

We hold each other for a long time and in his embrace, I know that I am safe. I am sure that our life ahead will bring its own challenges but I also know that there is absolutely no one else in this world that would be a better partner for me to face them with.

When Jackson pulls away from me, he asks, "Do you still want to go on this trip? We can postpone it, it's no problem at all."

I furrow my brow and look at him as if he has lost his mind.

"Are you crazy? Of course, I still want to go. We have our nuptials to celebrate."

THANK you for reading Tangled up in Love! If you enjoyed Jackson and Harley's story, I know that you will love Aiden and Ellie's.

It's a ""Decadent, delicious, & dangerously addictive!" romance you will not be able to put down. The entire series is out! 1-Click Black Edge NOW!

I don't belong here.

I'm in way over my head. But I have debts to pay.

They call my name. The spotlight is on. The auction starts.

Mr. Black is the highest bidder. He's dark, rich, and powerful. He likes to play games.

The only rule is there are no rules.

But it's just one night. **What's the worst that can happen?**

1-Click BLACK EDGE Now!

Start Reading Black Edge on the next page!

CHAPTER 1- ELLIE

WHEN THE INVITATION ARRIVES...

"Here it is! Here it is!" my roommate Caroline yells at the top of her lungs as she runs into my room.

We were friends all through Yale and we moved to New York together after graduation.

Even though I've known Caroline for what feels like a million years, I am still shocked by the exuberance of her voice. It's quite loud given the smallness of her body.

Caroline is one of those super skinny girls who can eat pretty much anything without gaining a pound.

Unfortunately, I am not that talented. In fact, my body seems to have the opposite gift. I can eat nothing but vegetables for a week straight, eat one slice of pizza, and gain a pound.

"What is it?" I ask, forcing myself to sit up.

It's noon and I'm still in bed.

My mother thinks I'm depressed and wants me to see her shrink.

She might be right, but I can't fathom the strength.

"The invitation!" Caroline says jumping in bed next to me.

I stare at her blankly.

And then suddenly it hits me.

This must be *the* invitation.

"You mean...it's..."

"Yes!" she screams and hugs me with excitement.

"Oh my God!" She gasps for air and pulls away from me almost as quickly.

"Hey, you know I didn't brush my teeth yet," I say turning my face away from hers.

"Well, what are you waiting for? Go brush them," she instructs.

Begrudgingly, I make my way to the bathroom.

We have been waiting for this invitation for some time now.

And by we, I mean Caroline.

I've just been playing along, pretending to care, not really expecting it to show up.

Without being able to contain her excitement,

Caroline bursts through the door when my mouth is still full of toothpaste.

She's jumping up and down, holding a box in her hand.

"Wait, what's that?" I mumble and wash my mouth out with water.

"This is it!" Caroline screeches and pulls me into the living room before I have a chance to wipe my mouth with a towel.

"But it's a box," I say staring at her.

"Okay, okay," Caroline takes a couple of deep yoga breaths, exhaling loudly.

She puts the box carefully on our dining room table. There's no address on it.

It looks something like a fancy gift box with a big monogrammed C in the middle.

Is the C for Caroline?

"Is this how it came? There's no address on it?" I ask.

"It was hand-delivered," Caroline whispers.

I hold my breath as she carefully removes the top part, revealing the satin and silk covered wood box inside.

The top of it is gold plated with whimsical twirls all around the edges, and the mirrored area is engraved with her full name.

Caroline Elizabeth Kennedy Spruce.

Underneath her name is a date, one week in the future. 8 PM.

We stare at it for a few moments until Caroline reaches for the elegant knob to open the box.

Inside, Caroline finds a custom monogram made of foil in gold on silk emblazoned on the inside of the flap cover.

There's also a folio covered in silk. Caroline carefully opens the folio and finds another foil monogram and the invitation.

The inside invitation is one layer, shimmer white, with gold writing.

"Is this for real? How many layers of invitation are there?" I ask.

But the presentation is definitely doing its job. We are both duly impressed.

"There's another knob," I say, pointing to the knob in front of the box.

I'm not sure how we had missed it before.

Caroline carefully pulls on this knob, revealing a drawer that holds the inserts (a card with directions and a response card).

"Oh my God, I can't go to this alone," Caroline mumbles, turning to me.

I stare blankly at her.

Getting invited to this party has been her dream ever since she found out about it from someone in the Cicada 17, a super-secret society at Yale.

"Look, here, it says that I can bring a friend," she yells out even though I'm standing right next to her.

"It probably says a date. A plus one?" I say.

"No, a friend. Girl preferred," Caroline reads off the invitation card.

That part of the invitation is in very small ink, as if someone made the person stick it on, without their express permission.

"I don't want to crash," I say.

Frankly, I don't really want to go.

These kind of upper-class events always make me feel a little bit uncomfortable.

"Hey, aren't you supposed to be at work?" I ask.

"Eh, I took a day off," Caroline says waving her arm. "I knew that the invitation would come today and I just couldn't deal with work. You know how it is."

I nod. Sort of.

Caroline and I seem like we come from the same world.

We both graduated from private school, we both went to Yale, and our parents belong to the same exclusive country club in Greenwich, Connecticut.

But we're not really that alike.

Caroline's family has had money for many generations going back to the railroads.

My parents were an average middle class family from Connecticut.

They were both teachers and our idea of summering was renting a 1-bedroom bungalow near Clearwater, FL for a week.

But then my parents got divorced when I was 8, and my mother started tutoring kids to make extra money.

The pay was the best in Greenwich, where parents paid more than $100 an hour.

And that's how she met, Mitch Willoughby, my stepfather.

He was a widower with a five-year old daughter who was not doing well after her mom's untimely death.

Even though Mom didn't usually tutor anyone younger than 12, she agreed to take a meeting with Mitch and his daughter because $200 an hour was too much to turn down.

Three months later, they were in love and six months later, he asked her to marry him on top of the Eiffel Tower.

They got married, when I was 11, in a huge 450-person ceremony in Nantucket.

So even though Caroline and I run in the same circles, we're not really from the same circle.

It has nothing to do with her, she's totally accepting, it's me.

I don't always feel like I belong.

Caroline majored in art-history at Yale, and she now works at an exclusive contemporary art gallery in Soho.

It's chic and tiny, featuring only 3 pieces of art at a time.

Ash, the owner - I'm not sure if that's her first or last name - mainly keeps the space as a showcase. What the gallery really specializes in is going to wealthy people's homes and choosing their art for them.

They're basically interior designers, but only for art.

None of the pieces sell for anything less than $200 grand, but Caroline's take home salary is about $21,000.

Clearly, not enough to pay for our 2 bedroom apartment in Chelsea.

Her parents cover her part of the rent and pay all of her other expenses.

Mine do too, of course.

Well, Mitch does.

I only make about $27,000 at my writer's

assistant job and that's obviously not covering my half of our $6,000 per month apartment.

So, what's the difference between me and Caroline?

I guess the only difference is that I feel bad about taking the money.

I have a $150,000 school loan from Yale that I don't want Mitch to pay for.

It's my loan and I'm going to pay for it myself, dammit.

Plus, unlike Caroline, I know that real people don't really live like this.

Real people like my dad, who is being pressured to sell the house for more than a million dollars that he and my mom bought back in the late 80's (the neighborhood has gone up in price and teachers now have to make way for tech entrepreneurs and real estate moguls).

"How can you just not go to work like that? Didn't you use all of your sick days flying to Costa Rica last month?" I ask.

"Eh, who cares? Ash totally understands. Besides, she totally owes me. If it weren't for me, she would've never closed that geek millionaire who had the hots for me and ended up buying close to a million dollars' worth of art for his new mansion."

Caroline does have a way with men.

She's fun and outgoing and perky.

The trick, she once told me, is to figure out exactly what the guy wants to hear.

Because a geek millionaire, as she calls anyone who has made money in tech, does not want to hear the same thing that a football player wants to hear.

And neither of them want to hear what a trust fund playboy wants to hear.

But Caroline isn't a gold digger.

Not at all.

Her family owns half the East Coast.

And when it comes to men, she just likes to have fun.

I look at the time.

It's my day off, but that doesn't mean that I want to spend it in bed in my pajamas, listening to Caroline obsessing over what she's going to wear.

No, today, is my day to actually get some writing done.

I'm going to Starbucks, getting a table in the back, near the bathroom, and am actually going to finish this short story that I've been working on for a month.

Or maybe start a new one.

I go to my room and start getting dressed.

I have to wear something comfortable, but something that's not exactly work clothes.

I hate how all of my clothes have suddenly become work clothes. It's like they've been tainted.

They remind me of work and I can't wear them out anymore on any other occasion. I'm not a big fan of my work, if you can't tell.

Caroline follows me into my room and plops down on my bed.

I take off my pajamas and pull on a pair of leggings.

Ever since these have become the trend, I find myself struggling to force myself into a pair of jeans.

They're just so comfortable!

"Okay, I've come to a decision," Caroline says. "You *have* to come with me!"

"Oh, I have to come with you?" I ask, incredulously. "Yeah, no, I don't think so."

"Oh c'mon! Please! Pretty please! It will be so much fun!"

"Actually, you can't make any of those promises. You have no idea what it will be," I say, putting on a long sleeve shirt and a sweater with a zipper in the front.

Layers are important during this time of year.

The leaves are changing colors, winds are picking up, and you never know if it's going to be one of those gorgeous warm, crisp New York days they like to feature in all those romantic comedies or a soggy, overcast dreary day that only shows up in one scene at the end when the two main characters fight or break up (but before they get back together again).

"Okay, yes, I see your point," Caroline says, sitting up and crossing her legs. "But here is what we *do* know. We do know that it's going to be amazing. I mean, look at the invitation. It's a freakin' box with engravings and everything!"

Usually, Caroline is much more eloquent and better at expressing herself.

"Okay, yes, the invitation is impressive," I admit.

"And as you know, the invitation is everything. I mean, it really sets the mood for the party. The event! And not just the mood. It establishes a certain expectation. And this box..."

"Yes, the invitation definitely sets up a certain expectation," I agree.

"So?"

"So?" I ask her back.

"Don't you want to find out what that expectation is?"

"No." I shake my head categorically.

"Okay. So what else do we know?" Caroline asks rhetorically as I pack away my Mac into my bag.

"I have to go, Caroline," I say.

"No, listen. The yacht. Of course, the yacht. How could I bury the lead like that?" She jumps up and down with excitement again.

"We also know that it's going to be this super exclusive event on a *yacht*! And not just some small 100 footer, but a *mega*-yacht."

I stare at her blankly, pretending to not be impressed.

When Caroline first found out about this party, through her ex-boyfriend, we spent days trying to figure out what made this event so special.

But given that neither of us have been on a yacht before, at least not a mega-yacht – we couldn't quite get it.

"You know the yacht is going to be amazing!"

"Yes, of course," I give in. "But that's why I'm sure that you're going to have a wonderful time by yourself. I have to go."

I grab my keys and toss them into the bag.

"Ellie," Caroline says.

The tone of her voice suddenly gets very serious, to match the grave expression on her face.

"Ellie, please. I don't think I can go by myself."

CHAPTER 2 - ELLIE

WHEN YOU HAVE COFFEE WITH A GUY YOU CAN'T HAVE...

And that's pretty much how I was roped into going.

You don't know Caroline, but if you did, the first thing you'd find out is that she is not one to take things seriously.

Nothing fazes her.

Nothing worries her.

Sometimes she is the most enlightened person on earth, other times she's the densest.

Most of the time, I'm jealous of the fact that she simply lives life in the present.

"So, you're going?" my friend Tom asks.

He brought me my pumpkin spice latte, the first one of the season!

I close my eyes and inhale it's sweet aroma before taking the first sip.

But even before its wonderful taste of cinnamon and nutmeg runs down my throat, Tom is already criticizing my decision.

"I can't believe you're actually going," he says.

"Oh my God, now I know it's officially fall," I change the subject.

"Was there actually such a thing as autumn before the pumpkin spice latte? I mean, I remember that we had falling leaves, changing colors, all that jazz, but without this...it's like Christmas without a Christmas tree."

"Ellie, it's a day after Labor Day," Tom rolls his eyes. "It's not fall yet."

I take another sip. "Oh yes, I do believe it is."

"Stop changing the subject," Tom takes a sip of his plain black coffee.

How he doesn't get bored with that thing, I'll never know.

But that's the thing about Tom.

He's reliable.

Always on time, never late.

It's nice. That's what I have always liked about him.

He's basically the opposite of Caroline in every way.

And that's what makes seeing him like this, as only a friend, so hard.

"Why are you going there? Can't Caroline go by herself?" Tom asks, looking straight into my eyes.

His hair has this annoying tendency of falling into his face just as he's making a point – as a way of accentuating it.

It's actually quite vexing especially given how irresistible it makes him look.

His eyes twinkle under the low light in the back of the Starbucks.

"I'm going as her plus one," I announce.

I make my voice extra perky on purpose.

So that it portrays excitement, rather than apprehensiveness, which is actually how I'm feeling over the whole thing.

"She's making you go as her plus one," Tom announces as a matter a fact. He knows me too well.

"I just don't get it, Ellie. I mean, why bother? It's a super yacht filled with filthy rich people. I mean, how fun can that party be?"

"Jealous much?" I ask.

"I'm not jealous at all!" He jumps back in his seat. "If that's what you think…"

He lets his words trail off and suddenly the conversation takes on a more serious mood.

"You don't have to worry, I'm not going to miss your engagement party," I say quietly. It's the weekend after I get back."

He shakes his head and insists that that's not what he's worried about.

"I just don't get it Ellie," he says.

You don't get it?

You don't get why I'm going?

I've had feelings for you for, what, two years now?

But the time was never right.

At first, I was with my boyfriend and the night of our breakup, you decided to kiss me.

You totally caught me off guard.

And after that long painful breakup, I wasn't ready for a relationship.

And you, my best friend, you weren't really a rebound contender.

And then, just as I was about to tell you how I felt, you spend the night with Carrie.

Beautiful, wealthy, witty Carrie. Carrie Warrenhouse, the current editor of BuzzPost, the online magazine where we both work, and the daughter of Edward Warrenhouse, the owner of BuzzPost.

Oh yeah, and on top of all that, you also started seeing her and then asked her to marry you.

And now you two are getting married on Valentine's Day.

And I'm really happy for you.

Really.

Truly.

The only problem is that I'm also in love with you.

And now, I don't know what the hell to do with all of this except get away from New York.

Even if it's just for a few days.

But of course, I can't say any of these things.

Especially the last part.

"This hasn't been the best summer," I say after a few moments. "And I just want to do something fun. Get out of town. Go to a party. Because that's all this is, a party."

"That's not what I heard," Tom says.

"What do you mean?"

"Ever since you told me you were going, I started looking into this event.

And the rumor is that it's not what it is."

I shake my head, roll my eyes.

"What? You don't believe me?" Tom asks incredulously.

I shake my head.

"Okay, what? What did you hear?"

"It's basically like a Playboy Mansion party on steroids. It's totally out of control. Like one big orgy."

"And you would know what a Playboy Mansion party is like," I joke.

"I'm being serious, Ellie. I'm not sure this is a good place for you. I mean, you're not Caroline."

"And what the hell does that mean?" I ask.

Now, I'm actually insulted.

At first, I was just listening because I thought he was being protective.

But now...

"What you don't think I'm fun enough? You don't think I like to have a good time?" I ask.

"That's not what I meant," Tom backtracks. I start to gather my stuff. "What are you doing?"

"No, you know what," I stop packing up my stuff. "I'm not leaving. You're leaving."

"Why?"

"Because I came here to write. I have work to do. I staked out this table and I'm not leaving until I have something written. I thought you wanted to have coffee with me. I thought we were friends. I didn't realize that you came here to chastise me about my decisions."

"That's not what I'm doing," Tom says, without getting out of his chair.

"You have to leave Tom. I want you to leave."

"I just don't understand what happened to us," he says getting up, reluctantly.

I stare at him as if he has lost his mind.

"You have no right to tell me what I can or can't do. You don't even have the right to tell your fiancée. Unless you don't want her to stay your fiancée for long."

"I'm not trying to tell you what to do, Ellie. I'm just worried. This super exclusive party on some mega-yacht, that's not you. That's not us."

"Not us? You've got to be kidding," I shake my head. "You graduated from Princeton, Tom. Your father is an attorney at one of the most prestigious law-firms in Boston. He has argued cases before the Supreme Court. You're going to marry the heir to the Warrenhouse fortune. I'm so sick and tired of your working class hero attitude, I can't even tell you. Now, are you going to leave or should I?"

The disappointment that I saw in Tom's eyes hurt me to my very soul.

But he had hurt me.

His engagement came completely out of left field.

I had asked him to give me some time after my breakup and after waiting for only two months, he started dating Carrie.

And then they moved in together. And then he asked her to marry him.

And throughout all that, he just sort of pretended that we were still friends.

Just like none of this ever happened.

I open my computer and stare at the half written story before me.

Earlier today, before Caroline, before Tom, I had all of these ideas.

I just couldn't wait to get started.

But now...I doubted that I could even spell my name right.

Staring at a non-moving blinker never fuels the writing juices.

I close my computer and look around the place.

All around me, people are laughing and talking.

Leggings and Uggs are back in season – even though the days are still warm and crispy.

It hasn't rained in close to a week and everyone's good mood seems to be energized by the bright rays of the afternoon sun.

Last spring, I was certain that Tom and I would get together over the summer and I would spend the fall falling in love with my best friend.

And now?

Now, he's engaged to someone else.

Not just someone else – my boss!

And we just had a fight over some stupid party that I don't even really want to go to.

He's right, of course.

It's not my style.

My family might have money, but that's not the world in which I'm comfortable.

I'm always standing on the sidelines and it's not going to be any different at this party.

But if I don't go now, after this, that means that I'm listening to him.

And he has no right to tell me what to do.

So, I have to go.

How did everything get so messed up?

CHAPTER 3 - ELLIE

WHEN YOU GO SHOPPING FOR THE PARTY OF A LIFETIME...

"What the hell are you still doing hanging out with that asshole?" Caroline asks dismissively.

We are in Elle's, a small boutique in Soho, where you can shop by appointment only.

I didn't even know these places existed until Caroline introduced me to the concept.

Caroline is not a fan of Tom.

They never got along, not since he called her an East Side snob at our junior year Christmas party at Yale and she called him a middle class poseur.

Neither insult was very creative, but their insults got better over the years as their hatred for each other grew.

You know how in the movies, two characters

who hate each other in the beginning always end up falling in love by the end?

Well, for a while, I actually thought that would happen to them.

If not fall in love, at least hook up. But no, they stayed steadfast in their hatred.

"That guy is such a tool. I mean, who the hell is he to tell you what to do anyway? It's not like you're his girlfriend," Caroline says placing a silver beaded bandage dress to her body and extending her right leg in front.

Caroline is definitely a knock out.

She's 5'10", 125 pounds with legs that go up to her chin.

In fact, from far away, she seems to be all blonde hair and legs and nothing else.

"I think he was just concerned, given all the stuff that is out there about this party."

"Okay, first of all, you have to stop calling it a party."

"Why? What is it?"

"It's not a party. It's like calling a wedding a party. Is it a party? Yes. But is it bigger than that."

"I had no idea that you were so sensitive to language. Fine. What do you want me to call it?'

"An experience," she announces, completely seriously.

"Are you kidding me? No way. There's no way I'm going to call it an experience."

We browse in silence for a few moments.

Some of the dresses and tops and shoes are pretty, some aren't.

I'm the first to admit that I do not have the vocabulary or knowledge to appreciate a place like this.

Now, Caroline on the other hand…

"Oh my God, I'm just in love with all these one of a kind pieces you have here," she says to the woman upfront who immediately starts to beam with pride.

"That's what we're going for."

"These statement bags and the detailing on these booties – agh! To die for, right?" Caroline says and they both turn to me.

"Yeah, totally," I agree blindly.

"And these high-end core pieces, I could just wear this every day!" Caroline pulls up a rather structured cream colored short sleeve shirt with a tassel hem and a boxy fit.

I'm not sure what makes that shirt a so-called core piece, but I go with the flow.

I'm out of my element and I know it.

"Okay, so what are we supposed to wear to this *experience* if we don't even know what's going to be going on there."

"I'm not exactly sure but definitely not jeans and t-shirts," Caroline says referring to my staple outfit. "But the invitation also said not to worry. They have all the necessities if we forget something."

As I continue to aimlessly browse, my mind starts to wander.

And goes back to Tom.

I met Tom at the Harvard-Yale game.

He was my roommate's boyfriend's high school best friend and he came up for the weekend to visit him.

We became friends immediately.

One smile from him, even on Skype, made all of my worries disappear.

He just sort of got me, the way no one really did.

After graduation, we applied to work a million different online magazines and news outlets, but BuzzPost was the one place that took both of us.

We didn't exactly plan to end up at the same place, but it was a nice coincidence.

He even asked if I wanted to be his roommate – but I had already agreed to room with Caroline.

He ended up in this crappy fourth floor walkup in Hell's Kitchen – one of the only buildings that they haven't gentrified yet.

So, the rent was still somewhat affordable. Like I said, Tom likes to think of himself as a working class hero even though his upbringing is far from it.

Whenever he came over to our place, he always made fun of how expensive the place was, but it was always in good fun.

At least, it felt like it at the time.

Now?

I'm not so sure anymore.

"Do you think that Tom is really going to get married?" I ask Caroline while we're changing.

She swings my curtain open in front of the whole store.

I'm topless, but luckily I'm facing away from her and the assistant is buried in her phone.

"What are you doing?" I shriek and pull the curtain closed.

"What are you thinking?" she demands.

I manage to grab a shirt and cover myself before Caroline pulls the curtain open again.

She is standing before me in only a bra and a matching pair of panties – completely confident and unapologetic.

I think she's my spirit animal.

"Who cares about Tom?" Caroline demands.

"I do," I say meekly.

"Well, you shouldn't. He's a dick. You are way

too good for him. I don't even understand what you see in him."

"He's my friend," I say as if that explains everything.

Caroline knows how long I've been in love with Tom.

She knows everything.

At times, I wish I hadn't been so open.

But other times, it's nice to have someone to talk to.

Even if she isn't exactly understanding.

"You can't just go around pining for him, Ellie. You can do so much better than him. You were with your ex and he just hung around waiting and waiting. Never telling you how he felt. Never making any grand gestures."

Caroline is big on gestures.

The grander the better.

She watches a lot of movies and she demands them of her dates.

And the funny thing is that you often get exactly what you ask from the world.

"I don't care about that," I say. "We were in the wrong place for each other.

I was with someone and then I wasn't ready to jump into another relationship right away.

And then...he and Carrie got together."

"There's no such thing as not the right time.

Life is what you make it, Ellie. You're in control of your life. And I hate the fact that you're acting like you're not the main character in your own movie."

"I don't even know what you're talking about," I say.

"All I'm saying is that you deserve someone who tells you how he feels. Someone who isn't afraid of rejection. Someone who isn't afraid to put it all out there."

"Maybe that's who you want," I say.

"And that's not who you want?" Caroline says taking a step back away from me.

I think about it for a moment.

"Well, no I wouldn't say that. It is who I want," I finally say. "But I had a boyfriend then. And Tom and I were friends. So I couldn't expect him to—"

"You couldn't expect him to put it all out there? Tell you how he feels and take the risk of getting hurt?" Caroline cuts me off.

I hate to admit it, but that's exactly what I want.

That's exactly what I wanted from him back then.

I didn't want him to just hang around being my friend, making me question my feelings for him.

And if he had done that, if he had told me how he felt about me earlier, before my awful breakup, then I would've jumped in.

I would've broken up with my ex immediately to be with him.

"So, is that what I should do now? Now that things are sort of reversed?" I ask.

"What do you mean?"

"I mean, now that he's the one in the relationship. Should I just put it all out there? Tell him how I feel. Leave it all on the table, so to speak."

Caroline takes a moment to think about this.

I appreciate it because I know how little she thinks of him.

"Because I don't know if I can," I add quietly.

"Maybe that's your answer right there," Caroline finally says. "If you did want him, really want him to be yours, then you wouldn't be able to not to. You'd have to tell him."

I go back into my dressing room and pull the curtain closed.

I look at myself in the mirror.

The pale girl with green eyes and long dark hair is a coward.

She is afraid of life.

Afraid to really live.

Would this ever change?

CHAPTER 4 - ELLIE

WHEN YOU DECIDE TO LIVE YOUR LIFE...

"Are you ready?" Caroline bursts into my room. "Our cab is downstairs."

No, I'm not ready.

Not at all.

But I'm going.

I take one last look in the mirror and grab my suitcase.

As the cab driver loads our bags into the trunk, Caroline takes my hand, giddy with excitement.

Excited is not how I would describe my state of being.

More like reluctant.

And terrified.

When I get into the cab, my stomach drops and I feel like I'm going to throw up.

But then the feeling passes.

"I can't believe this is actually happening," I say.

"I know, right? I'm so happy you're doing this with me, Ellie. I mean, really. I don't know if I could go by myself."

After ten minutes of meandering through the convoluted streets of lower Manhattan, the cab drops us off in front of a nondescript office building.

"Is the party here?" I ask.

Caroline shakes her head with a little smile on her face.

She knows something I don't know.

I can tell by that mischievous look on her face.

"What's going on?" I ask.

But she doesn't give in.

Instead, she just nudges me inside toward the security guard at the front desk.

She hands him a card, he nods, and shows us to the elevator.

"Top floor," he says.

When we reach the top floor, the elevator doors swing open on the roof and a strong gust of wind knocks into me.

Out of the corner of my eye, I see it.

The helicopter.

The blades are already going.

A man approaches us and takes our bags.

"What are we doing here?" I yell on top of my lungs.

But Caroline doesn't hear me.

I follow her inside the helicopter, ducking my head to make sure that I get in all in one piece.

A few minutes later, we take off.

We fly high above Manhattan, maneuvering past the buildings as if we're birds.

I've never been in a helicopter before and, a part of me, wishes that I'd had some time to process this beforehand.

"I didn't tell you because I thought you would freak," Caroline says into her headset.

She knows me too well.

She pulls out her phone and we pose for a few selfies.

"It's beautiful up here," I say looking out the window.

In the afternoon sun, the Manhattan skyline is breathtaking.

The yellowish red glow bounces off the glass buildings and shimmers in the twilight.

I don't know where we are going, but for the first time in a long time, I don't care.

I stay in the moment and enjoy it for everything it's worth.

Quickly the skyscrapers and the endless parade

of bridges disappear and all that remains below us is the glistening of the deep blue sea.

And then suddenly, somewhere in the distance I see it.

The yacht.

At first, it appears as barely a speck on the horizon.

But as we fly closer, it grows in size.

By the time we land, it seems to be the size of its own island.

***

A TALL, beautiful woman waves to us as we get off the helicopter.

She's holding a plate with glasses of champagne and nods to a man in a tuxedo next to her to take our bags.

"Wow, that was quite an entrance," Caroline says to me.

"Mr. Black knows how to welcome his guests," the woman says. "My name is Lizbeth and I am here to serve you."

Lizbeth shows us around the yacht and to our stateroom.

"There will be cocktails right outside when you're ready," Lizbeth said before leaving us alone.

As soon as she left, we grabbed hands and let out a big yelp.

"Oh my God! Can you believe this place?" Caroline asks.

"No, it's amazing," I say, running over to the balcony. The blueness of the ocean stretched out as far as the eye could see.

"Are you going to change for cocktails?" Caroline asks, sitting down at the vanity. "The helicopter did a number on my hair."

We both crack up laughing.

Neither of us have ever been on a helicopter before – let alone a boat this big.

I decide against a change of clothes – my Nordstrom leggings and polka dot blouse should do just fine for cocktail hour.

But I do slip off my pair of flats and put on a nice pair of pumps, to dress up the outfit a little bit.

While Caroline changes into her short black dress, I brush the tangles out of my hair and reapply my lipstick.

"Ready?" Caroline asks.

Can't wait to read more? **One-Click BLACK EDGE Now!**

ABOUT CHARLOTTE BYRD

Charlotte Byrd is the bestselling author of many contemporary romance novels. She lives in Southern California with her husband, son, and a crazy toy Australian Shepherd. She loves books, hot weather and crystal blue waters.

Write her here:
charlotte@charlotte-byrd.com
Check out her books here:
www.charlotte-byrd.com
Connect with her here:
www.facebook.com/charlottebyrdbooks
Instagram: @charlottebyrdbooks
Twitter: @ByrdAuthor
Facebook Group: Charlotte Byrd's Reader Club
Newsletter